CW00395105

EVERY FOX IS A RABID FOX

Harry Gallon

15.07.17

fernando -

thanks for the cover quote and for all the support!

EVERY FOX IS A RABID FOX

Harry Gallon

dead ink

94/100

dead ink

Copyright © Harry Gallon 2017
All rights reserved.

The right of Harry Gallon to be identified as the author of this work has been asserted by him in accordance with the Copyright, Designs and Patents Act 1988.

First published in Great Britain in 2017 by Dead Ink, an imprint of Cinder House Publishing Limited.

Paperback ISBN 9781911585060
Hardback ISBN 9781911585046

Printed and bound in Great Britain by Clays Ltd, St Ives plc.

www.deadinkbooks.com

CONTENTS

ONE

TWO

THREE

one

THE SECRET LIVES OF HIRED GUNS – PART ONE

All I can think about is killing pedestrians. Usually it's with a Bren gun. .303. Small rounds with longevity and long history leaving their mark. I want the dexterity. The curved, 30-round box magazine. I want to mount it on the front of a bus. In a bipod. Ball. Hydraulic gun turret. Bullet-proof glass. Wrist chain to handrails. No escape.

It may be central London that makes me think about killing pedestrians. It may be Kristin Scott Thomas or John Gielgud or Les Misérables. It could just as equally be Heisenberg Says Relax. DOT DOT DOT. And lunch at Pret A Manger. Sometimes it's the feeling of emptiness I get in the cove between my neck and shoulder, where a Thompson sub-machine gun should be. The later, military version: bolt on the side of the receiver. 20-rounds queuing for the chamber, .45 automatic cartridge, stub-nose. Sea of wooden stock thumping my rocky shore as every round leaves the muzzle, not really aiming, just sort of hoping to hit something fleshy.

My dead little sister, for instance. That would be messy.

My brother's dead too. I killed him. I used to get my eggs from him but I don't anymore because I killed him. He had a smallholding and garage in Essex with his wife. She has it by herself, now. They had fifteen chickens and a cockerel his wife kept threatening to kill. I could have had a sister but apparently I killed her too. I pushed her out of our mother's womb with a soft elbow and an overdeveloped god complex.

Or so my dead sister tells me.

To field-strip your Bren light machine gun you should do the following: remove the magazine and check that the chamber is empty. If the chamber is not empty, clear it. When the chamber is empty, remove the quick-detachable barrel. To remove the quick-detachable barrel, rotate the carrying handle upwards to disengage the barrel catch. Slide the barrel out and away from the receiver, then remove the captive push-pin at the back of the receiver in order to slide out the lower assembly. The lower assembly contains the bolt carrier, the gas piston and the recoil spring. Attached to the lower assembly are the shoulder stock (wooden), the grip (wooden) and the firing mechanism (trigger).

Remove the bipod. Clean all metal parts with a good brand of gun oil. My father recommends Youngs 303. It smells like soggy wood sheds and angry walks on Boxing Day.

The Bren gun is notably reliable. To reassemble, go backwards. Use the bipod to stabilise. Fire up to 500 rounds per minute in short bursts. Don't get distracted. Spraying wildly at moving targets from a number 76 at Oxford Circus. That's NOT how Gentleman Jim would have done it.

My uncle, Gentleman Jim, had HIV. But that couldn't have killed him. It's not the eighties. It's not even the nineties. It had to have been something else. The ghost of my sister, perhaps, draped upon me by our mother, who I know loved Jim but couldn't tell him, and so kept burning herself on the oven.

My brother stole Jim's motorcycle when he was fifteen. It was too heavy for him. He crashed it and broke his wrist.

Click.

Bone through skin.

It seems likely to have been my father's indifference to Gentleman Jim's disappearance that eventually did my uncle in. Or a gun in the right hands. Either way, there was always someone who had it in for Jim. Most of the time it was himself.

What we, my not-yet-dead brother (at least, back then), dead sister and I, knew, or thought we knew, about our uncle, we'd seen through a stranger's living room window.

It was this: our Uncle Jim pulling a *kukri* across the stranger's throat. He pulled the knife tenderly. He looked as though he really cared about the stranger, while he was cutting his oesophagus open. He looked as though he could've loved the stranger, as the stranger's blood bled on him. The look was in the gloves he wore. Black cotton gloves. Not black leather gloves. You'd have thought a hitman would use black leather gloves that were only lined with cotton. You'd have thought a hitman wouldn't have lingered after having pulled, so tenderly, a very sharp and historically charged tribal and military knife across a stranger's voice box.

It was so long ago, I can't even be sure that it happened.

The windows were double glazed. So my not-yet-dead older brother and my already-dead little sister couldn't have heard anything even if the vocal cords hadn't been cut. Even if the knife was inserted at the back of the stranger's ear, instead of under his chin, and drawn down the side of the stranger's neck to just above where the stranger's collar bone met the stranger's sternum, cutting his carotid artery.

Even if, I mean, the stranger had been given the chance to scream.

But Jim was a professional.

He held the stranger tenderly, and the stranger didn't gasp. He stared, with his mouth full, at Jim, whose expression said, 'It doesn't have to hurt.'

The stranger was lying on the floor of his living room. It was a wooden floor. The stranger's hands were fastened behind his back with a thick black cable tie. Veins were popping and he was squashing his own lungs with the weight of his fear; though most of that weight was being drained onto the reclaimed wood floor of his living room.

Gloves black, face bare. We saw all this through a powerful telescopic sight mounted on a bolt-action Browning .243. A good deer hunting rifle. Gentleman Jim's rifle. It had a bipod at the base of the barrel. Short wooden stock. Before he died and before I killed my brother but long after my father accidentally blew off part of his foot in a cadet training accident, Jim took us to a field, my brother and sister (dead) and I, where he taught us to shoot high-velocity. Jim rested the rifle on the bonnet of his Toyota pickup truck, pointed it at a target he'd already placed at the other end of the field about 100 metres away. When I fired, the kick made me cry. I don't know how my brother reacted.

We watched Jim with the knife and Jim with the stranger through the telescopic sight on Jim's rifle. Assassins like, we'd hoped, our uncle: confused at having, at least in our whispering, bedtime imagination, been hired to kill the same stranger as him.

As Jim.

We were hiding in a midnight fort. Lamplight torch dangling from a metre stick crossbeam, load-bearing pillow cases with sweet wrapper skirting boards, a duvet roof and eye-gouged windows. There were plastic soldiers all around us re-enacting Kelly's Heroes and wondering why our father's brother always brought his own meat round for supper. Wondering whether humans really did taste like pork.

'Like pigs?' I said to my brother, who shook his head in a very adult way.

'Like pigs,' said our sister, though only I could hear her.

I didn't know who to believe. My brother was shaking his

head, but if what my dead sister had said was correct, would it even matter if we'd been eating dead humans for dinner?

'Jim doesn't cut up his victims,' said my brother. 'He's not a serial killer. He's just good friends with a butcher. Gives him free cuts of meat, sometimes. For protection.'

'He's not a gangster,' said my sister. 'He works on a very high and stealthy commission.'

We were three children lost in a cemetery. Throughout our childhood, it seemed like death was always nearby, the way we'd fantasise about Gentleman Jim's disappearances, the weird men he'd associate with. The weapons. The knives in our mother's kitchen. And, despite my sister being cold as death, death felt safe and warm, in our pillow fort, while our parents slept and we'd wonder about what, exactly, our uncle really did get up to with that deer hunting rifle, and why he, such a handsome man (according to my mother), never brought any girls round.

'He pulled the knife across the throat,' said my brother. Torchlight storyteller (and alive for a few more years), 'tenderly, as though he was both sad and terribly happy. He pu-u-u-ulled the knife across his–'

'Throat.'

*

Our uncle, Gentleman Jim, kept the *kukri* knife in the bottom drawer of his desk. Whenever our father took us to visit him, his house always smelled like what I know now to be sex. His sofa sweaty. His bathroom bloody. His study smelled like electricity. His desk smelled like a heart beating outside its chest cavity, on the floor, in the corner, kicked there by whoever tore it out. Electrifying the pool of blood it lay in. Carbonated lightning. Jim's desk smelled like longing. It was where we, as two-and-a-half partially deceased children, imagined he conducted his nefarious business.

But we didn't have much to go on. He didn't have much of a kitchen, so he'd come to ours more often for meals, for our mother's burnt wrists, and our father's early exit for evening bell ringing at the church down the road, then a pint.

There were old model planes hanging above his desk. And another drawer to the left of his chair which, locked, contained (according to my brother, who had once previously looked into it through a strong telescopic sight mounted on his forearm), DVDs.

'What kind of DVDs?' I'd asked.

'Doesn't matter.'

'What kind of knife was it?'

'A *kukri*,' said my brother. 'The knife of the Gurkhas.'

'It's the one they have to cut themselves with every time they unsheathe it,' whispered my sister, so close my brother couldn't hear her.

We were lying still by the pillows for walls and bedroom architecture. Inside the leaf canopy, within the darkening cemetery. It was late. Midnight. We put the caps back over the scope on the rifle. Our deadly uncle was no longer visible through the stranger's living room window, and we'd assumed he'd taken the body into the bedroom, which was at the back of the house.

We disengaged the bolt and unloaded the rifle, just like how our uncle had shown us in that field on the bonnet of his pickup truck. We hadn't needed to fire a shot, so this time I didn't cry.

It was dark. Darker. We were hidden, pleasingly, inside the belly of a yew tree. Two warm hidden bodies and one dead one.

We approached the stranger's house slowly. The cemetery was part of a meadow on a hillside. The stranger's dog was waiting. The stranger's dog had come home while we were packing the rifle back into its case and loading it into the boot of Jim's pickup truck which we imagined we'd stolen but which, given the location of our bedtime hideout, was just our father's armchair. Handbrake kickback. Lazyboy feet on the dashboard. Toyota flatbed, matt black in midnight camouflage but Jim never took it on jobs.

That, at least, made sense.

We approached the stranger's house. Two dressed up children and their dead sister's ghost, one long winter coat, deep collar round my neck because, as the youngest, I was the lightest and therefore on top. Next was my sister, though technically lighter because she came out of our mother a few months earlier than me, grey, limp, unable to breathe, and she sat on the shoulders of our five-years-older brother, wet coat cuffs at his ankles. I hadn't wanted to approach the house. Dark sky, bats swooping and air too thick to breathe. I was small, a Minpin. Living on sibling branches with Christmas tree lighting. But intrigue had got the better of me. Why DID our Uncle Jim keep a *kukri* knife, with its notch for blood run-off at the base of the blade, and those locked away DVDs of what could, I'd then assumed, only have been sick, perverted recordings of his professional hitman murders?

'They DID have strange men on the covers,' said my brother, winding me up.

The stranger's dog was at the door.

The knife had belonged to our grandfather. He'd taken it from the body of a dead Nepalese soldier in North Africa. Passed it down through the family artery. Each successive generation another notch to add to the list of successfully confused children.

The cemetery smelled like the ocean on a sunny day. And I was the head on a very unconvincing body, knocking on the door of a stranger's house where a man in his late 30s had just committed murder.

'It's not murder,' said my brother. 'Uncle Jim's a hitman.'

I looked at my sister. 'It's not murder when it comes with commission,' she said.

'Does killing strangers for a living pay well?' I asked.

'Idiot,' said my brother. 'Of course it pays well.'

'Then why does he never go shopping?'

'What?'

'If Jim has a lot of money for killing somebody bad. They're all bad, right? Was the stranger bad? If Jim has a lot of money, why does he never buy food?'

My sister said, 'Because he eats them afterwards, remember?'

'Shut up,' said my brother, but not to her. 'Who're you talking to?' he asked me, still under the light of the torch, the metre stick crossbeam it hung from, the duvet for ceiling now lurching in, threatening to send us back to bed. 'Our dead little sister,' I shouldn't have said.

I knocked on the front door of the stranger's house. The stranger's dog was sitting by a small sculpture of a frog on the step next to the door. It was looking at our sister's torso. The stranger's dog was a spaniel. The frog began casting a shadow from the porch light, which clicked on as we approached. The dog was too low down to set it off. The dog had already knocked but had not yet received a reply. The door opened. Gentleman Jim, as we'd come to know him in this guise – as executioner and advocate of suicide – was drying his hands on a tea towel. He wasn't smiling. The tea towel had the self-portraits of primary school kids printed on it. They were smiling, mostly.

Jim's fly was undone.

The stranger's dog tried to get passed his legs but his legs were iron bars barring entry into what, clearly, had become a dungeon. The dog barked. My brother swayed. His kneecaps were only ten-years-old. I said, 'We've been watching you from our cemetery bush. I mean, from a yew tree. Up there, in the cemetery,' all three successively turning and pointing back up the hill. Jim said nothing. Something coughed. It was my belly. It was half-past-eleven and we had school in the morning. 'We were watching you through a powerful 16x50 scope mounted on a bolt-action Browning .243.'

'That's a good rifle,' said Gentleman Jim, maybe.

My brother creaked under the strain.

'Who is we?' Jim said.

'My associates and me,' I said. Jim's moustache twitched. He had a moustache when we were children. Or he always had a moustache. It made him look like a waiter from a restaurant that existed in an era before cigarettes caused cancer and AIDS started killing relationships and people overcame their fear of accidentally killing people by actually killing people. It was an era in which Gentleman Jim looked as though he always should have lived.

'Clearly we've been hired to, um, kill the same stranger,' I said.

Jim said, 'I don't know what you're talking about.' His shirt was unbuttoned at the collar and untucked, just a little, at the waist.

The dog whined.

'We heard grunting,' I said. 'We saw you, through our powerful rifle-mounted telescopic sight, holding a strange man's head with one hand. He was on his hands and his knees, facing you. You were holding something approximately six-and-a-half inches long in the other.'

'Sixteen inches.'

My brother coughed. 'It's practically a machete.'

'What's that?' said Jim.

'No one,' I said. 'I mean, nothing. You want to watch out the police don't catch you walking around with a knife that big.'

My sister giggled.

Jim said, 'Is that a threat?'

There was a pause.

'Have you ever been deer hunting?' I said. Gentleman Jim looked unimpressed. He raised his eyes and let out a sigh and said, 'I think you'd better leave.' And with that, slowly, my brother turned, then my sister turned, so, by force of queer momentum I, too, turned, swaying jaggedly, stumbling back up the hill past the university I'd later attend (before, even, my brother became dead), up the hill to the cemetery, the reality of our beds, dissatisfied in knowing that we knew nothing more about what our dead-eyed uncle did to strange men after dark, though pleased that we, all two-and-a-half of us, had succeeded in making an otherwise redoubtable man sweat.

Just then, on that hill, the sky lit up. Lightning torch with all its bolts – all five volts of them – splitting the calm of our hidden evening: 'Boys, go back to bed.'

It was our father.

It was work in the morning.

'What about the dog?' I said quietly, in the few moments we had left.

'He went inside after we left the story,' said my brother, 'and found his master propped up in a chair, stains all over the upholstery.'

'What kind of stains?'

'Don't worry. He was just propped up in an armchair, bled dry, eyes closed, face white as a duvet cover.'

'What duvet cover?'

Another pause. Ears cocked for footfall on stairs. My brother lay rigid, silent.

'Did it call the police?' I asked. 'The dog?'

'No,' said my brother. 'He called the stranger's wife.'

'He had a wife?' said our dead sister, giggling. 'That's embarrassing.'

'How do you know the dog was a boy?' I said.

'I think the dog was a girl,' said our sister. 'Girls are smarter.'

'No,' said my brother, with some years left alive. 'The dog was a boy. The frog was a girl. And she'd seen everything.'

WHAT ABOUT THE KNIFE IN HIS DRAWER?

Three barely existent children. Three barely distinguishable minutes since our father crashed feet through the ceiling and tore down our pillow fort and ordered us back through our bedroom door. We'd tried asking our father what Gentleman Jim's real job was numerous times. We'd tried asking him in McDonald's but he'd been too distracted because I couldn't finish my fries. Too much milkshake. No answer. 'That toy stinks of a deep fat fryer,' in the car on the drive home.

We'd tried asking him in the car on other occasions, and he'd sigh and rub his temples with both hands off the wheel and his eyes closed as though he was trying to play the Five Second Game with the two of us (my sister didn't count because she was already dead). We weren't scared. The Five Second Game hadn't hurt anyone before. He was an adult, a man in control. And he was never that good at the game because he only managed to count up to three.

When he opened his eyes again, he'd say something like, 'You've asked me that before.' Or he'd say something like, 'You know that question's boring.' Or he'd say nothing with his mouth and say something with his hand like SMACK. Reaching round into the back to where either one of us would be sitting. It didn't matter which one took it. We'd even fight between us to get the seat behind his because it offered a little more protection, but still his arm could reach.

When it rained, the car wouldn't start. Those were days of relief.

In the morning my father ate cornflakes. Tired, having been kept up every night by his children.

Tired.

Cornflakes.

'Dad?'

It would usually be my brother, while our mother was packing our lunches in silence, daydreaming about divorce.

'Dad?'

Sip of instant coffee.

'Dad?'

While I dipped my soldiers.

'Dad?'

And the yolk was destroyed.

Dad, who was preparing himself for the agony of leaving the house again.

'Dad,' said my brother, 'what does Unc–'

'He's a debt collector,' said our father. 'He goes to people's houses and takes money from them. And when they ask too many questions about why he does what he does, he gets tired and has to sit down. And where do you think he sits?'

'On top of them?'

'That's right. He sits on their chest until their every last breath has gone.'

Then there'd be a pause. An awkward ruffle of hair or a funny face. The oven door would slam to break it up and everyone would look at mother.

'What about the knife in his drawer?' I'd ask.

'We don't talk about that,' said Mother, rubbing her arms.

'Is it true it belonged to our grandfather? Is it true our grandfather got it from a dead Gurkha in North Africa? Is it–'

'That's enough,' said our mother, who'd wanted a daughter so badly.

IF YOU COULD KILL SOMEONE, HOW WOULD YOU DO IT?

'If you could kill someone, how would you do it?'

'Here we go,' says Willow before sipping her vodka cranberry. Same colour as her hair. I was ten minutes early, bought it for her before she arrived. 'Is that really what you want me to tell my housemates when I get home? That we talked about murdering people?' The drink is still close to her mouth. She's teasing a small piece of ice, shaking the glass so slightly she could be trembling. She's not trembling. It's Willow. 'What will you tell them, then?' I ask.

'That I'm done dating men,' she says.

'This is a date?'

She raises her eyes. Seems hours ago she was hugging me. Didn't expect that. 'How've you been?'

'Okay, thanks.'

'Have you been here long?'

'I got here ten minutes early.'

'Why'd you get here ten minutes early?

'So I could buy you a drink and settle into my surroundings.'

'Same old vodka cranberry.'

'I got here early so I could take some cocaine in the toilet.'

She wipes her left nostril with her thumb.

'So, not that okay, then' she says, looking at me like I'm a victim. 'You don't have to pretend with me. It's not like we don't know each other well.'

I take a drink. Mine's a lager.

'I'd use a high-velocity rifle,' I say. 'A Lee-Enfield .303, maybe, or a Mauser Kar98K. Something with history. A proven track record. But it depends on who I was killing. Knives are personal; explosives cinematic. Out of the question. Anyway,' pausing for a moment to drink again, 'you said you're a florist now?'

'I am a florist,' she says, shrugging. 'So much for the English degree.'

I laugh. That's good. That means I don't have to buy her flowers to say thanks for meeting me. Or it means I have to worry twice as much.

'Japanese cherry blossom,' she says.

'I'm sorry?'

'Before you freak out,' she says. 'Sit there in silence for two-and-a-half minutes trying to work out if my favourite flower is the same as when we were going out. And no, you don't ever have to buy some for me. I still care about you. I want to make sure you know that you can talk to me.'

'Isn't that a tree?'

'They're all the same to me,' she says. 'As long as they're pink.'

'Like your hair?'

'No,' she says. 'My hair is cranberry.'

She crunches the ice.

There's a pause.

'Do you need another drink?' I ask.

'I think I do,' she says, hand in purse. Denim skirt. Sensible heels for a quick getaway. Thirty inch dark wood reclaimed table with a red glass candle holder between us. Wax on the surface. Wax on her fingers. Wax, bored, wax, waiting. Possible hand across the table, it'll be alright, you'll get through this.

'No, it's fine,' I tell her. 'I know the bartender.' Walking to the bar carefully, little drunk having necked a 25ml whisky in the ten minutes I nervously waited, careful not to trip, checking flies not undone and dick not hanging out, no shit on shoes and, wiping nose, no residue.

'Why are you here,' I say to the bartender, tall, bob, who is also my dead little sister.

'I thought you missed me,' she says, 'for a moment. What

with my new hair and, well, age. Look,' she says, holding her chest, 'I've got boobs.'

'Do you think this is a good idea?'

'It's the same thing I've been doing every night,' she says, 'since you found my body in the downstairs bathroom. Remember that?'

I rub my head. 'Pint of lager and a vodka cranberry,' I tell her.

'Fine,' she says, 'but it's not going to be free.'

'Who's she?' asks Willow.

'The bartender?' I ask, putting down the vodka cranberry. 'She's my dead twin sister,' sitting down with the lager for me.

'I thought you killed her when you were both babies?' she says. Her straw lies in a cranberry puddle next to the candle holder. I wipe my right nostril. 'What did you use, a high-velocity rifle?'

'Very funny,' I say, looking back at the bartender who'd turned back into a stranger. 'Actually, it was an elbow.'

'You haven't changed,' says Willow.

There's a pause.

'How is your mother, by the way? I can't imagine what she's–'

'In shock, but she'll be okay.'

'I don't think a parent can recover from a thing like that.'

'Hmm.'

'And your uncle as well.'

'Can we talk about something else?'

'I'm sorry,' she says, then doesn't say anything for a few minutes.

'If I was going to kill someone,' she says, 'you, for instance, I'd go on a date with you, to an overpriced bar which stinks of aftershave and ambition. I'd make you pay for all my drinks and an expensive meal, even if I wasn't hungry. Then, when I'd decided it was over, I'd kiss you.'

'Why would you kiss me if you're done dating men?'

'It's not meant to be romantic. It's business. Besides, I am dating someone.'

'A man?'

'Yes.'

'How long?'

'Three months. I'm seeing him later, actually.'

I nod. 'How is it?'

'Easy.'

'Ouch.'

'Well, we're older now, aren't we?'

'I always thought we might try it again one day.'

'Shut up and listen,' she says. 'If I wanted to kill you I'd kiss you. And you'd kiss me too, of course. But you'd do so without realising that there was poison in my lipstick. That my lips were toxic. It'd be sweet. You'd die comfortably in your sleep, hours after we'd parted. But you wouldn't, ever, be sleeping beside me again.'

'We tried that already.'

'Don't remind me.'

'Fuck me,' I say, 'that's so personal. And besides, you're wrong.'

'How?'

'You don't know me anymore.'

'And,' she says, 'that's exactly how it should stay.'

SAYS MY DEAD LITTLE SISTER

Not little, because she was conceived at the same time as me. Technically older, actually, because she came out early, and dead. And that's how she'd always be: like rubber. Like one of those fake newborn babies you see on TV. In films. Rubber. Limbs giggling like the tits her lips never sucked from.

I'm already coming down.

If you drop those limbs they bounce. If my parents dropped her when she was pulled out, dead, and placed into their arms, if they'd dropped her, just to see what dropping a baby felt like without doing any harm because its cream-egg-sized heart wasn't beating, would she have bounced? I wonder.

Boing.

A bouncy ball bouncing off the walls.

Did she even have bones?

I could never grip and choke her like a twin brother is, play fighting, supposed to.

Boing.

Calcium melts at around 860 degrees. Bones do not melt like rubber. As a porous matrix of mineral crystals they fall apart, resembling billions of hands holding each other tight, then tenderly letting go. My brother's porous matrix of mineral crystals disintegrated just like that. Decorated a puddle of rubber as though lemon zest on a cheesecake, while my sister and I were watching. Blood racing on adrenaline. And then everything slowed down. Blood vessels rubbernecking, like cars at the side of a motorway.

Boing.

Rubber melts at around 180 degrees. Cars bounce. 'Can you feel that?' says my sister.

'Feel what?' I ask.

'The blood,' she says, 'pumping through your head.'

'I think that's all I can feel,' I tell her, as I lie in my bed with my head between the mattress and the paralysing prospect of getting up.

'Can you hear it?' she says.

'It sounds like a–'

'It sounds like when you put your ear to a seashell. When you listen to the sea. Remember when we last went to the sea? In France? The last family holiday. The cottage in Brittany, the one with the locked door on the upstairs landing and the stuffed pygmy alligator?'

'Yes.'

'Do you think there were bodies behind that door?'

'Shut up.'

'Our dead brother trod on a weaver fish and had to soak his foot in hot water.'

'It sounds like my–'

'And our father left early on business. What is it you think he was doing? Do you think it concerned Gentleman Jim?'

I've stopped listening.

My sister tells me to breathe.

My sister says, 'Do you smell it?'

Your heart keeps missing beats. And your temples are throbbing. Two tiny hands, a baby's hands, are pulling them together from the inside to crush your brain, drip out of your nose and onto the bed sheet. My phone is ringing and I can't even summon the strength to put it on silent. I just want–

'What's that?' says my sister.

'I want to–'

'Hide in a fort made of pillows?' she says. 'Did you have a nice time with Willow, by the way? Did you reminisce?'

They stood in silence outside the pub as he rolled another cigarette, she shivering in the wind, wiping her nose on her scarf. He moved deliberately slow, making her wait. When he eventually lit the cigarette and put the red lighter back in his jacket pocket she started to walk down the street. But he took her by the arm, stopping her, pulling her towards him. Then he kissed her. His cigarette between his fingers, his hand on her cheek.

'Fuck me,' says my sister, rolling her eyes. 'I know you left her,' she says, 'feeling paranoid about death, brain haemorrhaging, after taking all that cocaine in the toilet and scaring her off, again, with all your talk of murdering.'

'It's not murder when you're given permission.'

'And now you can't sleep, deeply uncertain as you are about what potential you have left for any future habitation on this earth. Head buried and buried further. Veins jerking so hard, working your jaw muscles so hard you can feel your–'

Wait.

'–temples swelling. Expanding. Contracting like metal rapidly cooling. Car chassis on an icy road. In flames. Rattling heart–'

Let me count–

'–beat, heartbeat, heart beating the bedsprings that shake. Waiting for the police to finally take you away. Do you think it'd fix anything, anyway, if you got back together? Go out for dinner? Italian? Go back to work? Make money while she decorates this tiny flat with flowers? Be normal again? Ignore me, again? You're not at university anymore. You're fully grown. It's okay.'

–to one.

'It's okay, feels okay, doesn't it, when you're surrounded by people who think you bring something to the table. It's just–'

Two.

'–that it's only when you're alone again, that you see–'
Three.
'–just how bare the table is.'
Four.
'Its edges are cliffs. And spaghetti is a rope that stops halfway.'
Five.

DIGGING DIRT – PART ONE

Digging dirt can refer to two things. Both involve literal dirt digging. And gravel. Neither involves uncovering harmful information with the intention of blackmailing someone close to you.

No one blackmails Gentleman Jim.

We spent so much time digging dirt as kids. This was before I killed my brother but after I'd elbowed myself suitable space inside our mother, whose daughter came out early and bloody and dead.

My father wanted to call me Romulus.
An overstated baby.

Digging dirt: the soundtrack shooting up your arm in a shiver. A sting. As though jumping into a freezing cold river during winter or taking a piss after having contracted a urinary tract infection. Digging dirt: our mother perched on a birthing chair after a sixteen-hour labour, aiming downwards into a large potty so that her remaining twin baby could eventually march out vertically, in combat boots, having already committed his first atrocity.
I had a fringe.

My sister wasn't haunting me then like she does now. It didn't take long, though. I'd fall over and scrape the skin off my nose at school, or get my dick caught in my fly or be unable to answer a question in maths. Usually that'd be attributed to her. The invisible cause. Or karma, of sorts. Grey and wet and buried. But never crying on the back seat on the way to school with dad's unhappy, rough, tradesman's hand smacking her knee. She was growing. She grew with me. I asked my mother, 'Do you know who Remus was?' at the dinner table one evening after a Year 4 introduction to Ancient Rome.

My mother said, 'He was a man with a vision,' as she eyed my father, who was always doing something. Who was always inadvertently tearing down my mother's walls with his tongue and trying hard to build new ones out of his sons.

Digging dirt: my brother took our father's rusting 12 bore shotgun cartridges into the kitchen. They were an heirloom. Dug out from dirt of closets and understairs cupboards filled with familial ugliness. They, like the *kukri* knife that we would dream and dream and fantasise about sliding across the stranger's throat in the night, belonged to our grandfather, long late from whatever cancer, possibly of the throat, if not the bruises he left on his eldest son's skin with a belt; who hid his whisky behind curtains and broadened his gene pool horizons by establishing his family as a military institution that no one, actually, would join.

His sons straight and narrow and his wife long suffering.

'He'd stand at the fence round our garden,' my father told us often, 'when we were stationed abroad with his regiment, in various countries suffering varying degrees of unrest. During riots and guerrillas and fighting for independence, he'd stand with his shotgun, in case anyone broke into our compound. And when the stone-throwing subsided and the yelling subsided and the shadows in the evening creeping along the perimeter garden fence subsided he'd come inside for the whisky he'd hidden earlier on behind every curtain in the house–'

Gulp.

'–and he'd–'

'Yes?' said my brother.

'Tell us about the gun?' asked my dead sister.

'–he'd–'

'What, Dad?'

As if we were there, on the veranda.

SMACK!

'Was it something Jim did?'

Never.

A little later, when I and my brother and spectral dead sister were teenagers, we'd ask our father, feeling the clarity of some years behind us, 'What did Jim ever do to make our grandfather hi–'

'Not right now.'

'But what about the letters in the attic? The possible love affairs he could have had?'

'Boys,' from our mother, always open ear through the kitchen door from where she could hear us polishing guns, 'don't bother your father,' pushing herself into a corner, stirring the mixing bowl. Preparing dessert. 'Another bin cake?' our father would blurt out. To deride her. To keep his whisky not behind the curtain but inside of her. 'My favourite. How many have you chucked away this time?'

'They're too young,' her eyes would tell him, from some corner of the kitchen or while stoking the fire or when administering the terrier's insulin injection.

'Psst,' Dad whispering so she couldn't hear, 'he used to hit him because he fancied bo–.'

'Stop!'

Somewhere, a cough.

'Your mother's baking a cake, boys,' our father would say loudly instead. 'You can have some after lunch.'

'Bit ironic,' said my brother, still thinking about Jim, 'given that he'd sent you and Jim to boarding school.'

'Never mind that now,' said our father. 'Hey, did I ever tell you about the time I found a machine gun washed up on a beach?' In fact, he did. It was mangled. 'I'd always wanted to find a gold doubloon,' said our father, who cleaned his shotgun with the same fingers he used to touch our mother.

'Youngs 303,' he'd say. 'That's what it needs,' wielding a shoulder stock and foregrip. 'Give it a good clean.'

Smells like pheasant, death and family.

Again, digging dirt: my brother went into the understairs cupboard, to where the big metal gun cabinet is still fastened with rawl bolts to the outside wall, facing away from the cupboard door, behind some camouflage jackets, and took five rusting 12 bore shotgun cartridges out of a damp cardboard box and into the kitchen.

Our parents were at church in the village: Mother flirting with evening mass, Father ringing the bells.

My brother placed the rusting 12 bore cartridges onto the kitchen table next to a chopping board. It was the garlic and onion chopping board. It was the ace-of-spades-shaped chopping board. My brother placed one cartridge onto the chopping board then covered it with a tea towel. He said, 'Hand me a large, sharp kitchen knife.' And I handed him a large, sharp kitchen knife. 'Wouldn't it be better to do this in Dad's shed?' I said.

'No,' said my not-yet-dead brother.

'Do it in Dad's shed,' said our sister, dead, who whispered in my ear: 'He'll know that you went in there. That you used his tools. His workbench and vice and his hacksaw. He'll catch you and smack you, just like he does in the car.'

'The only way to get away with using dad's tools,' said my not-yet-but-possibly-soon-because-he's-cutting-open-a-shotgun-cartridge-dead brother, 'is if we do this wrong and set the rusting percussion cap off, igniting the powder, propelling the shot, blowing our hands off and bleeding to death. That way he couldn't punish us.' My brother paused, thought, then said, 'Actually, I think he still would.'

'You wouldn't dare,' said our sister. 'Not like you killed me. Maybe take off some digits, a hand or three? You have four between you. Just remember.'

'What?' I asked her.

'Remember–'

'Who're you talking to?' said my brother.

'–to turn your head away.'

I turned my head away and said, 'It'd be better to empty the shot out first.' My brother concurred. With one hand he held the tea towel over the percussion cap, as if all the stains of our mother's cooking could protect him from an explosion. With the other he cut the crimp off the end of the cartridge, emptied the metal ball bearings into a dirty coffee mug by the sink, removed the wad and emptied the explosive charge into a clean tea cup on the dresser. Each time he cut, pressing down carefully with the kitchen knife, he turned his head towards me, so that at least I'd see the look in his eye if, somehow, the powder (smokeless, so you can see the fall of your bird) ignited, expanded, exploded outward and took off however much of his thirteen-year-old body was in the way.

I'd see it again.

Soon.

In the silence that followed my still-alive brother took a hammer and a nail. They were our father's hammer and nail. They came from his quick access hammer and nail drawer in the dresser. There was also a light bulb drawer and a battery drawer and a 'Do not go in there' drawer, but that one was in the bathroom and belonged exclusively to our mother.

He hammered the nail, gently, into one of the disconnected percussion caps–

Tap.

–rendering it useless.

Then he repeated the procedure on the four remaining rusting 12 bore shotgun cartridges until there were five empty cartridges with five deactivated percussion caps in front of us, five lots of ball-bearing shot sitting in a coffee mug, five discarded wads and a great huge pile of smokeless explosive charge plopped in a clean tea cup he then placed on the ace-of-spades-shaped chopping board. The powder (smokeless) wasn't really powder, more a lot of very thin paper-like squares, similar to cheap lino tiles or acid tabs.

'Smells weird,' I said.

'Like garlic and onion,' said my brother, who then took the clean tea cup and emptied the tabs into one deactivated cartridge. He tamped the tabs down with the back of a ballpoint pen, then added some more.

'Go and get your tin,' he told me.

So I went and got my tin.

I kept my tin under my bed.

No one was supposed to know about my tin.

It was an ammunition tin (200 rounds). It had 1942 stamped on the side, and it opened with a clasp. 'How'd you know about my tin?' I asked.

'We share a bedroom, idiot.'

My brother opened my tin and took out a French banger. The last one left over from the family holiday we'd all dragged ourselves through a year previously.

'I don't want him having those,' our mother had said to our father, who'd given me the money. 'He's a growing boy,' my father said back at her. 'He should be allowed to destroy things.'

My brother took out the banger, pulled out the green fuse (waterproof) and put it on the chopping board. Then he snapped the banger in two with his fingers, emptied the powder inside it (this time it really was powder) into the decommissioned shotgun cartridge. Then he took some kitchen roll and stuffed it into the top, covered it with a lot of electrical tape, poked a hole through the tape with the nail, inserted the fuse through the hole until the end of it touched the explosive, put the whole thing back down on the table, smiled and said, 'Now we have a grenade.'

DIGGING DIRT – PART TWO

For a long time I couldn't stop thinking about burning things down. As a child. As a student. I wanted to burn down every house that I lived in. With my parents, before they broke up. With Willow, before we did. That's why digging dirt was so appealing. It takes a lot of heat to set dirt on fire. More heat than is needed to burn down a house. Dirt wasn't as flammable back then. Seeing my suddenly-dead, hopefully-dead, older brother's body fat combusting in midair before it hit the ground changed all that.

Drip.

Drip.

Drip.

Many years earlier I suffered a bad bike crash. We'd dug the dirt and built the jumps and I pedalled fast down the path we'd made through the woods and then I was lying on my back, chest crushed by a large branch jutting out from a tree at the edge of the run-up. Blunt branch, like buffers at the end of a railway line.

Thump.

I had a habit of tilting sideways in midair. Over jumps we'd dug out of dirt. Left great canyons of earth in some farmer's field.

Thump.

Listing like a ship. Listing like my head would list in my eventual London bed, listening to the bedsprings sing with the pump pump pumping blood of heart through brain.

'Sit up, you idiot,' my still-alive brother said to me. With water (bottled) and a hand on my back, other hand dropping the bottle, unclasping the clasp of my helmet.

It was bright red, with barbed wire printed on it.

*

'Sit up now, you piece of shit,' my long dead sister hisses at me. 'Sit up and stand up and look up at the smoke.' Something's burning. 'Oh, something's always burning in London.'

'Is it the Shard?' I say. You can see the Shard from one of the windows in my flat. 'Wouldn't it be wonderful if the Shard just blew up?'

'Only if you were in it,' says my sister. Mine. Because our brother is dead and she's all I've got left. 'And yet–'

'Yes?' she says, while I'm waltzing, hungover, to and from the bathroom, the kitchen, the cupboards, the bin. I sank a bottle of wine last night. Again.

'–why doesn't he follow me around like you do?' I ask her. 'I killed him too, didn't I?'

'Maybe he doesn't think that's true,' she says, floating, as though perched on an open branch end, waiting for me to crash my bike. 'Maybe he thinks it's your father's fault? He's the one who taught you the Five Second Game, after all.'

Wait.

'Maybe he never believed in an afterlife. In heaven or hell or whatever else there might be. Maybe his body just burned away, and you've only yourself to blame for my being here.'

Okay.

Digging dirt: piles of earth, like the gravel we dredged from the waste area beside the watercress beds in the winter, by the river near our childhood home, which had ceased to flow and left dozens of trout to suffocate.

We upped our game.

Now we had a grenade.

Our father cleaning his father's BSA double-barrelled (side-by-side) 12 bore shotgun (the same one from the guerrilla stories) on the kitchen table, our mother in the kitchen with–

'Ah, another bin cake, wonderful,' from Father, hands covered in gun oil. Oily hands all over our mother, disarming every sense that she possessed until he drove her to–

Well, yes, but we're not quite there yet.

To strip your double-barrelled 12 bore shotgun, first remove the forward stock. Then break the barrels and cock the firing pins. Remove the barrels from the rear stock and trigger mechanism. Do not pull the triggers. Lay the barrels on some newspaper. Handle all metal with an oiled rag. Youngs 303 is preferable. Pull the barrels through in this order:

With a phosphor bronze brush (point down for best results).

With a wire loop (and an oiled tissue attached to it).

With a wool mop.

The phosphor bronze brush makes a mess (hence the newspaper). Use an old toothbrush to scrub the action, trigger and break mechanism. Reverse to reassemble. Do not pull the triggers.

*

Digging dirt by the empty concrete reservoir in the field behind our house. Its roof had caved on so we covered half of it with a few sheets of corrugated iron. Piled wood chips in from behind the farm buildings where our father left logs he'd cut from fallen trees. My brother, saving up all his pocket money for new suspension forks for his bike. Our dead little sister throwing sticks between the spokes of our wheels.

'Do you feel it?' she says to me now. 'That thumping in your chest? It's not the blunt tree trunk you swerved into. It's your heart struggling to beat.'

I'm going to die.

'Your brother doesn't haunt you because –'

'Why?'

'–he–'

'Please.'

'–hates–'

'I need–'

'–you.'

What do I need? To know why I chose to close my eyes at that exact moment. To know why I didn't just blow my head off, instead, with the little .410 that my father gave me, the one that'd once belonged to Uncle Jim. Five seconds. Don't rush it. Up the stakes if the weather is shit. And if it's dark, turn the lights off. If the moon is bright, you won't need them anyway. Suits always had suited my brother, but our mother would've definitely preferred a daughter.

On the day we burned down the barn my brother and I arrived in the woods at the top of the field behind our house and found that the dirt we'd dug to jump our bikes over had been flattened. Our canyons filled in. Our footprints rolled and the old shovels we'd stowed in a tree root rabbit hole removed, snapped and discarded. Our dirt trod flat told a secret. The remains of our spades were broken bones, the frames of our bikes scattered skeletons that lay prostrate on the topsoil.

Wheels spinning.

It was a sunny day. The air smelled like rapeseed. The earth smelled like cow shit. The world smelled like adolescent sex. We could see the heat shimmering, cheap, on the road above the village our parents had, once, insisted we all live in together.

'Better for bringing up children,' said Father, a mover; not Mother, who'd had to quit the shitty little town she'd grown up in to raise his–

Cough.

–her children. No longer moving (unless you count into stagnation, though that was already inhabited).

Above the village you could see for miles. All the houses and the school building lay warm in a little valley beside a chalk-bed-clear river. There were farm buildings dotted here and there. We knew the farmer whose land we'd been digging on. He was a friend of our father's. They rang the church bells together, evenings. Sank pints. Dad had built a downstairs bathroom in an annexe off his house. The annexe was for the farmer's mother, who was dying. We'd already had to knock on his door and 'Excuse me, can we have our spades back' several times before.

And he returned them, with a 'Don't do it again.'

'And don't do it again.'

'And again.'

So, really, it was our fault.

'But we have a grenade, now,' repeated my brother, holding a broken shovel in one hand and the bomb we'd made in the other.

'Go and strap it to one of his cows,' said our sister.

I told her, 'Shut up.'

'Then go and burn down his barn,' she said, which is what my brother, still young, was going to suggest anyway, short of posting it through his letter box, which we decided not to do because he had a daughter who was our age (roughly), and she was quite nice at school, despite smelling of Cheesestrings.

'Do we throw it like a grenade?' I asked my brother, once we'd cycled to the barn at the top of the village.

'We light it first,' said my brother. And he did, lit it with a half-inched cigarette lighter, threw, then hid next to me behind a couple of elder trees. The barn was full of dry straw and hot asbestos, it being summer, the beams so rusting the colour of dried blood. Oh wow, how it all went up, how it snapped, crackled and popped like breakfast.

A few hours later, our mother stood rabid at the door, like an earthquake, feet at the corners and arms at the sides, shaking the foundations of the farmer who wagged the fingers of one hand like podgy pink dildos, while with the other he held a dead fox.

'They done it,' he said.

The fox knew it.

'They done it alright,' he said. 'They've been digging up my land all summer.'

My sister stood giggling behind Mother. Always behind Mother. She never saw Mother. Her eyes never opened. I don't suppose my mother even cried when the doctor told her that one of her twins was missing. Still, she wasn't about to let this village green stranger place arson on the only children she had left.

'How dare you,' she said.

And DARE you.

'OUT!'

Our sister, wet with dried blood and placenta, hoping we were done for, looked bored.

The police must've found the percussion cap. We knew that asbestos is poisonous when it burns, but we'd no idea that, when heated, it would explode. You could see it from the hill on the other side of the valley. We knew because that's where we watched it from, having gone the long way round.

Collected shovels. Collected spades. Suspected arson. Imminent repercussion. Leaflets left by the neighbourhood watch and the village association through letter boxes warning good citizens that yobs and vagrants, probably from one of the nearby council estates, were about. But ammunition was already littering their lives. And besides, it only made a loud fizz then sort of burnt out before we left. 'Not packed tight enough,' my brother said later that evening after the farmer had left and our mother had sat down to read and wait for our father to get home from work. My brother went searching for closure in the understairs cupboard, to where the metal gun cabinet is still fixed to the outside wall with rawl bolts and covered with old camouflage coats. He took the damp box of old rusting 12 bore cartridges that, once, had belonged to our grandfather and–

'Fuck sake,' he said. 'There aren't enough left.'

THE CURE FOR LOVE

I lay in the bath for three hours this morning, thinking about the stranger's wife. And the *kukri* knife. And the dog barking in the frog-like shadow. And what the police think they're doing, not yet having arrested anyone for all the small deaths connected to my uncle over the years.

'But you finally managed to get out of the house,' says Willow. My pillow to be dry on. To apologise to and to sigh on. 'Have you eaten?' she says.

'Yes.'

'And your dead little sister?'

'She's at home folding oven pizza boxes in half. And old milk bottles and orange juice cartons. She's building a tower out of the recycling.'

'The Tower of Babel in your recycling bin?'

'That's right. She wants to climb to heaven.'

Willow laughs. Willow humours me. Willow doesn't ask questions about the haunting. She's heard enough about it already. She's concerned, but she doesn't want to press me.

'She's washing out pots of hummus,' I say, 'and draining jars of pickled dill cucumbers.'

Laying foundations of glass. And plastic that buckles in half when you pour boiling water on it.

'Well, good,' says Willow as we walk together through the park in the approach to the dark of a dead evening, coffees to go, silent as drones but more conspicuous. And Willow's the siren in the distance while I just keep walking, eyes following the childish cries vying on scooters, banking heavily to avoid toddlers and parents and a schoolgirl with long braided hair who hasn't noticed that the bottle of Diet Coke in her blazer pocket is leaking heavily and trailing a long line behind her, like petrol.

I start thumbing my lighter. I could be the cause. Willow looks forward determinedly to reduce the gravity of the looks she shoots my way, occasionally, point-blank; corner-eye glances that don't improve the quality of my mental state, nor her ability to see my life now for what it really is (an epilogue), but rather which betray to me the fact that she, clearly, has no idea how to talk to me anymore. We're older. Everything's on the edge of flammable and I'm the one holding the lighter.

I can see this bothering her. I can see her trying to care. She once knew me, knew me well, feels obliged. I get it. A child goes by on a small bike, loudly. Easy target. Back of the head, off his bike and into the duckweed stream next to the path we're following.

Willow drifts, a whale. Look up and she's a passenger jet. Four engines, more debris. A Boeing 747, or an AirBus A380. Drifting between clouds, through sea. And I'm a bottom feeder. Except the difference here is that her undercarriage, as she comes into land, isn't dangling like some great mammalian phallus from her blubber. It's still up inside her. And if she stays with me much longer we're both going to crash.

I want to apologise.

'My father–'

'What?'

Asks Willow.

'My father tried calling me earlier. When my sister started folding those oven pizza boxes and milk bottles and orange juice cartons.'

'Did you answer?' says Willow.

'I was in the bath.'

'Oh yeah.'

'For three hours.'

'You must've been very wrinkly.'

'He left a message.'

'Look at the size of the stick that dog's got,' says Willow, laughing a little while a pigeon creeps over like a troop-carrying glider and I thumb my lighter some more. 'Wants me to go see him,' I tell her.

'I think I might be pregnant,' she says.

'What?'

'I said–'

'Well, that's, uh, great.'

She stops. We're on the path that runs diagonally through the centre of the park, approaching the ponds, the fountain, the–

'Why've you stopped? I ask.

Willow looks at me. Willow says, 'Really? I could've fucked up my life and that's all you've got to say?' She shakes her head, smiles. 'I suppose I don't know what I expected.'

'Alright then, you're a fucking idiot.'

Pause.

'Aren't you on the pill?'

'No.'

'Morning after?'

'Yes.'

'Then why worry?'

'I threw up this morning,' she says.

'When?'

It's a big stick.

'Probably about an hour-and-fifty-seven minutes into your bath.'

Three-and-a-half feet.

'My housemate kept feeding the cat feta cheese. He was cutting it into cubes and putting them onto a plate.'

'Was it the green plate?'

'Yes,' she says. 'Sorry. I'd had a superfood smoothie. Spinach, avocado and kiwi. And the cat's tongue kept making weird noises.'

'So take another.'

'Smoothie?'

I roll my eyes. 'Another pill, for fuck sake.'

'Why are you being a dick?' she says. 'I've been trying to make you feel better.'

I cough. We carry on walking. 'Have you told your boyfriend?'

'He's not my boyfriend.'

'What happened?'

'Nothing, he's just not my boyfriend.'

'I'm pretty sure I'm sterile,' I say.

'From the accident?' she says. 'Is that possible?' My left foot and left shoe keep rubbing together. Dry humping each other. Heel swelling so I have a slight limp. The wind makes my nose run and I keep checking to make sure it's not blood. 'Why'd your housemate give the cat cheese?' I ask.

'His girlfriend dumped him. Now we can't listen to sad songs in the kitchen.'

'Did he cry?'

'He was more upset when David Bowie died.'

'Cat get halloumi?'

'Something like that,' she says. 'Look, I'm working this afternoon but I'm around later if you want to get another drink.'

THE FIVE SECOND GAME – PART ONE

There are two versions of the Five Second Game. The first one involves a shotgun. The second one involves a car. Those are the main tools you need to play the Five Second Game, though of course there are other things on the list. For the first version, these include: a good pair of boots, camouflage trousers and jacket, dark, fingerless gloves, a camouflage hat and a face mask (that, too, should preferably be camouflage).

There are no straight lines in nature.

There are no skin-coloured trees.

These, the other things you need, also include, for the second version of the Five Second Game: enough petrol to operate a car, some friends, some cans of lager and a bag of weed.

The items on these lists are surplus. You don't actually need them to successfully play the Five Second Game, either version. In fact you should be alone. If you're not alone, you may accidentally kill someone. And that's not the idea. The idea is to almost kill yourself. To come within a slip of the foot to pulling the trigger.

Boom.

And within three-and-a-half feet of hitting SMACK that tree at the side of the road.

My father was an early advocate of the second version of the Five Second Game: closing your eyes while driving, seeing if you can count to five before you either A) lose your nerve, or B) die.

This can also be done at night.

You don't have to close your eyes.

You simply turn off your lights.

Version two is a selfish game. There's likely to be collateral. My father said that Gentleman Jim invented it when they were kids, because the machine guns and rifles they'd been given to play with in the Combined Cadet Force at boarding school were only ever loaded with blanks and they weren't allowed to point them at the other boys, the ones who gave them birthday bumps each year. And maybe Jim wanted to kill them. And maybe Jim wanted to die. But I can't understand why he'd put my father, his younger brother, in the passenger seat, and try.

You pick up the kid whose birthday it is by the legs and the arms so his arse hangs down in a squatting position. Then you drop him. Then you lift him.

Then you drop him.

He's fourteen.

He's fifteen.

He's stealing a car with his younger brother. He's light as a feather because you outnumber him. 'I don't care if you look at pornography,' said his father, at the table, during school holidays, 'as long as it's not gay.' They were working class boys, really. They didn't belong there, in public school. They closed their eyes. They drove as fast as they could. Only–

'Only what?' I ask my sister, who's changing the bins.

'Only, Gentleman Jim, our uncle, never actually closed his eyes. He loved his brother too much to risk his life. Funny–'

'Please.'

'–how you, the younger, too, take after your father.'

'What do you mean?' I ask her.

The recycling's a real mess.

'Oh,' she says, sorting tea bags and eggshells, 'you'll see.'

*

I lied before. Or rather, I didn't tell the whole truth. Version one is selfish too. It goes like this: put the shotgun under your chin. Count to one.

Two.

Three.

Four.

You're still alive. You're younger. You had all the camouflage gear beforehand, when your father wouldn't let you take the real guns out, so you, me, we're digging dirt with our hands, building fence-panel pillboxes and constructing artery trenches to play soldiers in. Making war in the old watercress bed gravel pits, with bb guns for arms instead. They sting. My dead brother, who was still my not-yet-dead brother back then, invented one particularly unsettling role-play game in which one of us would play a downed pilot, armed only with a pen knife and a spring-powered toy pistol we'd somehow convinced our mother to buy us from a mail order catalogue. The pilot would find somewhere in the woods behind our house to hide, while the other, usually my alive older brother, would patrol in search of the man his imaginary comrades in an imaginary air force had shot down. And, since he'd be armed with a battery-powered toy machine gun that fired one-hundred-and-fifty plastic ball bearings per minute, capture him easily, bring him (usually me) back to the camp we'd dug in the gravel pits, and torture him.

To torture your younger brother you make him squat, arms extended, palms down, then lay a long, heavy branch across his arms. If he drops the branch, he has to dig dirt.

And dig.

And dig.

Our father had a deal with the farmer whose barn we'd burnt down. The farmer said we could shoot all the pests on his land, in exchange for having the pests on his land shot. But no pigeon, rabbit or crow had ever thrown a homemade hand grenade into an asbestos barn filled with straw before. So when I first played the Five Second Game (version one), I almost ridded him of his greatest foe. Our father was on the other side of the field with the pigeon call, flushing the birds down towards me. I was standing in a bush beneath an old yew tree at the top of the down – wild flowers, dry earth, rolled fields below and the smell of burnt wood – with an old .410 that had belonged to Gentleman Jim: rusty, with a worn old hammer and flecks of white paint on the stock, loaded, upturned and the end of the barrel cradling the butt of my chin.

'You should have pulled the trigger,' says my delightfully dead little sister. 'You should've pulled the trigger and saved your brother's life.'

'It's too late for that now,' I tell her, at the window of my flatblock tower.

'Our father would've thought you'd just shot a bird. Or tried to. He'd have called you on that little walkie-talkie you used and heard you gurgling.'

'Gurgling?'

'Yes, gurgling. With blood sloshing out of your mouth, or something. Thick and slow and dehydrated. Like cum from your third wank of the day. Because you, a fuck-up from an early age, couldn't even blow your own head off right. Christ,' she says, 'first it was me, then it was him. When will it end?'

I tell her to fuck off.

She's screaming, 'You're a plate licker!'

'It was our brother, alive, who threw that grenade.'

'And our mother who denied it,' she says.

'She wasn't your mother,' I tell her, high up in the tower but alone and alone and alone, 'little one, sister. You didn't even slide out of her. You, yes, you didn't even bounce off the ground.'

'You pushed me,' she says.

'So?'

'You closed your eyes and–'

Pray for lightning.

'Did nothing? I did nothing as you were sucked back into the lining of her womb.'

The vanishing twin.

'You're a syndrome,' I tell her, looking out of the window and aiming down the sights of an imaginary Lee-Enfield No. 4–

Bolt open.

Bolt closed.

–at the pedestrians crossing the common. 'Did you know our, I mean MY, father almost blew off his foot with a Lee-Enfield? It was during a training camp with the cadets.'

She's rolling her eyes. She's banging her drum. The tower sprouting out of the recycling bin is leaning threateningly.

He was at public school at the time. Deported from the family table. Gentleman Jim went too, to relinquish ploughs and chain harrows for pips and cap badges. A family theme.

If he drops the branch in the watercress beds by the stream, he has to dig.

And dig.

And dig.

'I'll straighten you out,' said my grandfather to Jim, with a smack to him, his head and slurp behind the whisky curtain and a mother (not mine, yet) who went to the downstairs bathroom to throw up.

Her body was rejecting her.

'Really?' I ask my sister, still clicking bolts and wondering how long it's been since I left my flat. 'Yes,' she tells me. 'Like yours. Your grandmother could feel something inside her. And no, it wasn't the corpse of a daughter.' My grandmother said nothing while my grandfather beat his son. And Gentleman Jim, the man always inside him, said nothing while it happened. That's where he got his name from. Maybe. Not necessarily from the way in which he collected those debts.

'By sitting on borrowers' chests?'

'That's right, yes,' says my sister. 'By keeping his mouth shut. Really shut. And not ever crying. Not even letting our father, his younger brother, see the bruising.'

He only opened himself up to men who had good, righteous and rigid ideas to put in him.

'I'll straighten you out,' said an officer of the army, not a father, after hearing the rumours that his oldest son was–

'So he sent him to an all-boys school?'

'I know,' sister giggling. 'Anyway, you were going to tell me–'

'About our father? When he was younger? And his brother wasn't dead, either? And he wasn't on the verge of shooting himself in the foot? Yes, he shot himself in the foot with a Lee-Enfield No. 4. That's the later war model. It has a protruding barrel at the end of the stock and the sight was redesigned to feature a rear receiver aperture and an additional ladder aperture that could be flipped up. More accurate than mid-barrel sights. It was also–'

'Yawn.'

'You don't have to be here, you know,' I tell my sister. 'You don't live here. You don't live.'

'Then who writes your shopping list?' she says. 'And who throws your eggshells away? I'm making your life appear normal. I'm keeping you alive.' She gets a toenail between her teeth. 'For now.'

'Why?'

'Because you know that no one can love you. And you don't yet deserve the relief that you think you'll get if you die.'

Pause.

'–lighter,' I say. 'It was also lighter than the version before.'

The Lee-Enfield No. 4 holds 10 rounds. High capacity for a bolt-action rifle. All 10 rounds can be fired off with accurate effect in one minute by a properly trained solder. But boys are not soldiers. They're also not children. They cannot be left to convalesce. They must be put to some form of training. Load up some rifles with blank ammunition. Shoot yourself in the foot in the hope that the empty cartridge casing may splinter enough to puncture your boot, then hope that the wound is bad enough to get you sent home to a mother too busy throwing up to listen and a father who jokes about chemical castration every time your brother mentions enjoying rugby lessons.

"Just don't enjoy them too much."

*

Shotgun ammunition is expensive. My mother didn't go to the downstairs toilet to throw up her own parasites in an attempt to escape. She just made cakes. But then, our father didn't beat us. He merely teased us, in spite of Gentleman Jim, who may have died of a self-inflicted gunshot wound to the head. Revenge, or repentance, for a string of dead strangers. Or just one confused, unfaithful, husband, who had a fetish for black cotton gloves, and men.

I only played version one, the Five Second Game, once. The

adrenaline was too much. I took my chin off the barrel, leant the gun against a tree. Leant the gun against my mother who got married too young; against my grandmother who made the mistake of telling her husband about that time she kissed another girl in an Anderson shelter, during the Blitz. Oh, he didn't like that one bit. I leant the gun against the tree.

And had a wank–

BANG.

–then mopped it up with a dock leaf. The vanishing twin, reabsorbed. But no tree is the colour of skin.

When my father, all camouflaged and face masked, arrived, he said, 'I was hiding up by the remains of that barn. Looks like arson to me. Did you get anything, by the way? I heard a shot.'

'I dropped my gun, Dad,' I said. 'I'm sorry.'

'Listen: you should ALWAYS leave the safety on when your gun isn't in the firing position. That's why it's so close to your thumb – so you can click it off at the last minute, right before pulling the trigger.'

Click.

'Jesus,' said my father. 'You're not hurt, are you?'

'No.'

'Maybe you're too young for this after all. Christ, I hate it when your mother's right.'

'We don't have to tell her,' I said.

My father smiled.

There was a pause.

And there is a pause. My dead little sister is writing another list.

My father and I walked back to the car. We'd left it in the farmer's yard. My father had picked up the old .410, wiped off the dirt, broken the barrel and removed the empty cartridge.

'Dad?' I said.

'Uh huh?'

'When'll I be old enough to drive?'

'Not for a few years yet. Why?'

'No reason.'

'Come on. Let's go find your brother,' he said, shaking his head. 'Kelly's Heroes is on this afternoon, and your mother's made bin cake again.'

Harry Gallon

WHEN I MET MY DEAD BABY SISTER

In the middle of the night I heard her crying. It was the first time. I was very young. She woke me up. I hadn't been in a particularly deep sleep to begin with. I'd shot a rabbit and when I walked over to it I saw that it was covered with fleas. Most of the fleas were on its long rabbit ears. Some were on its neck. I couldn't sleep that well because my scalp kept itching. Also, I had a fear of house fires. A fear of house fires. A fear of our house burning down every night. But not staying burnt. Reforming each day. Burning down, building up, over and over again. I wouldn't let myself sleep too deeply in case the house caught on fire. In case the soot in the chimney combusted. Created a vertical wind tunnel. In case a spark from a piece of pine was thrown up on the carpet by the dog's bed. In the night. Parents asleep. Brother asleep. In case Gentleman Jim, parents not yet sleeping, all digesting the aftermath of red wine and curry, didn't put out one of his cigarettes properly before he went home.

I slept in acts, punctured with intervals.

I heard her crying. Or I heard someone crying. And the sound of the crying pre-empted the second interval that night.

At the first interval, I woke up as usual. Act One had gone exactly as planned. My brother was asleep in his bed on the other side of our shared room. Our door was open. Only open a little. Light from the hallway shone under it and around it and the house was silent and warm and the air smelled like air, not fire or blood which is metallic. Back then I dreamed of internal combustion. Of tiny infinite spontaneous explosions occurring all around me.

*

I saw the rabbit in my sights. My father and I had been walking back down the track from the field with the old concrete reservoir in it, towards the farmer's yard where we'd left the car. I asked my father if Gentleman Jim was coming for lunch. My father said, 'Your uncle's out of town at the moment,' then looked away. The track was muddy and ran in funny zigzags from the top of the down where the wild flowers were, by the bush in which I'd propped my gun and had a wank, earlier.

My father stopped and put his arm out in front of me. I wobbled because I was standing on a flint. My father, arm out straight, said nothing. He pointed, and his finger, rather than his mouth, spoke, 'Rabbit.'

*

The house was silent. First interval. I sat up, went out onto the landing, down the stairs which were steep. I checked all the rooms in the dark. I checked the bin in the kitchen, and the boiler by the downstairs toilet in the downstairs bathroom. I filled the black Mars Bar cup with water and drank it by the back porch. I always drank my interval water from the black Mars Bar cup because when the water was gone I could see the reflection of my eyes at the bottom, and they didn't know who they were looking back at. I held them open, wide, and drank another.

I drank water before I slept in order to wake back up. A healthy human bladder can hold around sixteen ounces of urine comfortably for two to five hours. Less for a child, which I was. I drank three cups at eight o'clock. The first interval was at half-eleven. At half-eleven, after checking all rooms in the dark, I drank two more cups. Second interval at half-two. I refilled the cup a third time and poured it into the rusty old Parkray stove, just in case.

Then I turned the lights on, looked around to make sure everything was as still as it sounded. When I turned the lights off I ran quietly up the stairs, panicky in anticipation of being grabbed by the leg, if the eyes at the bottom of the black Mars Bar cup had grown a body and legs and were following me back up to bed.

*

When I lifted the shotgun and tucked it into my shoulder and steadied my breathing and remembered to keep both eyes open and pulled the trigger as I exhaled, not only because I'd been told to (this wasn't a rifle) but because it made me feel lethal, nothing happened. After finding me with my hands stuck to dock leaves–

'You alright, son? Stung yourself or something?'

–my father had broken the gun, removed the spent cartridge and carried it down the track himself. He'd seen the rabbit and handed the gun back and instructed, 'Now, tuck it–'

Like this?

'–into your shoulder.'

First kill.

'You see it?'

Not first.

'You see 'im?'

Not sister.

'Breathe steadily–'

I'd hoped it was a him.

'–and gently pull the trigger.'

Click.

We'd both forgotten to reload the .410. I had a cartridge belt, leather, round my waist. All live. All shiny percussion caps and bright red plastic staring up at me like the eyes of a spider.

*

In the middle of the night I heard a baby crying. At first I didn't think it was a baby crying. At first I thought it was my mother. But in the darkness and the warm silence and after finding the body which I knew I'd find anyway, though I don't know how, then yes, there had always been a baby crying.

I woke up.

I'd been lying on my back.

My face was cold.

I sniffed the air. It smelled like gun oil.

Click

It was 1:35am. The ache in my bladder was still only gentle. I didn't have to stagger when I got out of bed, legs crossing, I just got up and went out onto the landing where the light shone. I stood by my parent's door, heard nothing more, at first thinking, yes, Mother. Muffled crying. Must've been. It wasn't high. But my mother doesn't cry. She bakes cakes instead, and says everything's okay despite the burnt edges. She spends Sundays in the kitchen, slow cooking lunch and projecting. 'It's good beef. Isn't it a good piece of beef? It's a very, very good piece of beef. And the leeks–'

'The leeks?'

'The creamed leeks. They're really, very good.'

'Very creamy. Very–'

'Cheesy?'

'Yes dear. Creamy and cheesy. Now pass the salt.'

I followed the crying past my parents' room. It wasn't my mother, silent, mother, tolerant. Father, fingers owning her. Didn't cry, except occasionally when she'd read magazines and think of all the French beaches she was sure she'd never see. I followed the crying downstairs to the bathroom. Turned on the light. Feet shuffling. Floor tiled. My father had always aspired to have under-floor heating. He likes to have warm feet and heat rising from somewhere other than his chest. The crying was loud in my head but quiet everywhere else. The house was dark and silent. I trod in something wet on the tiled floor as I entered the bathroom.

It was blood.

Blood under the sink by the toilet by the boiler above a tiny body lying in a pool of blood. Thin blood. Menstrual blood. Blood which formed canals in the channels between the floor tiles, unheated.

When I turned on the light and looked down I saw a little grey rubbery thing trembling in the puddle. I touched it, turned it over and saw that it was a girl, sister, daughter, rubber limbs giggling like broken, couldn't control them and eyes screaming nightmares behind lids that would never open.

Is it true that babies can survive underwater? In a birthing pool? Because their lungs have not yet been exposed to the air?

I was looking down and couldn't decide who was the nightmare: her or me. The sound of her crying, which was distant (though she was lying at my feet), felt less immediate than the feeling that her sound was flaying my skin. That the blood on the floor had come from me. And I knew it. Red as tomato purée. Crawling up my shins like mud on Boxing Day.

I began scratching myself.

Clawing its way up.

And up.

And open.

*

The bubble broken. The breach closed but the head split jaggedly open. After the first click, when I'd pulled the trigger and realised that the gun was empty, my father took it from me, carefully, extending the trigger guard to cock the gun and break the barrel. I, equally cautious, took a cartridge from my belt and passed it to him. He pushed the cartridge into the breach. It was green all around us. Morning frost slowly melting in the light that came through the trees. Flies in the sun through the branches. Daddy-long-legs irritating spiders' webs. My father and I watching the rabbit on the other side of a rusting barbed wire fence where the track, at the end, thirty yards, zigzagged right down the hill. The wind was coming towards us. My father clicked the gun shut and handed it back.

It was an easy shot. The rabbit, when I lifted the gun to my shoulder, had already seen us. It stood up on its hind legs. And that's when I fired.

The kick from a .410 shotgun is affectionate. Like having your neck bitten during sex.

The other end is, predictably, less flirtatious.

The rabbit was thrown into the air by its nervous system, which had become disconnected from its brain after the shot pulverised its head.

The skull was cracked through and leaking.

Still looked like a rabbit, though, so I didn't feel too sick.

It was the bubble of blood that did that. Father, kneeling, broke a necessary neck, which forced a final rabbit struggle, and a thick red blood bubble out of what remained of the animal's nose.

Pop.

*

Standing in the bathroom puddle, I knew it was my sister. I knew it was my sister because I knew it was my sister. She was something I'd always missed and had pulled that trigger for, hoping, too, to be reabsorbed.

*

It was sunny on the track. The broken mounds of tarmac dumped by the farmer whose barn my not-yet-dead big brother and I burned down. I was sweating and sweating her out.

Two deaths in one day.

I said, 'Sister.'

To the rabbit.

I said this quietly.

A whisper.

My father didn't hear.

Pop.

Then, 'Sister,' to the little grey thing under the sink by the downstairs toilet next to the boiler.

Dead.

'Sister?'

She, on her tiny back, stopped crying with that and–

'Are you there?'

–opened her eyes.

I turned quickly and vomited.

When I woke in the morning I'd pissed myself. And my mother was mopping bin cake up off the floor.

THE GREEN PLATE

'We stood in silence outside the restaurant while I rolled another cigarette.'

'You gave your first one to a homeless guy.'

'That's right. And you kept wiping your nose.'

'I'm pretty sure I wanted to go.'

'Wait. Wiping your nose, and I was moving deliberately slowly, making you wait.'

'Don't remind me. That's one of the reasons why I wanted to leave. And you weren't nearly as cool as you thought.'

'I said wait, Willow. Cold. Wait in the cold as I lit my cigarette then put the lighter back in my jacket pocket. Or–'

'What?'

'–was it my trouser pocket?'

'Can we just go inside, please?'

'Wait. WAIT. Hit that button.'

'What button?'

'That button.'

'Why?'

'For the heat lamps.'

'What heat lamps?'

'The heat lamps above your head.'

'What was it you did, or said, then? Get–'

'It was my jacket.'

'–on with it.'

'Definitely my jacket. That's right. Anyway–'

'You kissed me.'

'And then we dated for two years.'

'Three.'

'Can't have been that bad a first date.' Willow stands up. 'Hey, what's your rush?'

'I want another drink.'

'You can't drink when you're pregnant.'

'I'm not pregnant.'

'Remember how you always used to think you were pregnant?'

'Remember how you always used to drink too much and annoy me?'

'Like right now?'

'Exactly. You're fucked.'

'I'm boring. Home's drunk. And mad. My sister is bad at organising the deconstructed Tetra Paks. The recycling bin's been a complete mess all day.'

'You know, this whole sister thing was funnier when we were students. But now, if people hear you talk about ghosts like they're real, they'll think you've lost it.' She goes inside. Suddenly I feel very heavy. And empty, as though there's no breath inside me. When she comes back with another drink she sits and says, 'I didn't mean to sound like a dick just now. People have weird ways of coping with things, don't they.'

'I don't want to go home,' I tell her, looking down at my foot, which is shaking.

'Then,' says Willow, coughing as she rolls a cigarette, 'come to mine instead.'

'The problem is, I don't really want to be anywhere.'

'My housemate's away. We can drink his wine.'

'Have you cleaned the green plate yet?' I ask.

'We're not getting any coke in,' Willow says before hitting the button. 'And besides, I'm meant to be pregnant, aren't I?' She smiles.

'You're absolutely fucking right. I'm sorry. Have you taken the test?'

'Not yet.'

'Well,' I say, 'you're glowing.'

She laughs. 'Definitely just the heat lamp,' she says, wrapping her scarf around her neck. 'Hold on.'

I'm sitting on the bench. Threat of carrion airstrike imminent. Can't get anything up, least of all myself. Too much blood squirting round in my head, my belly, my chest. Bouncing the springs. Lying alone. Spending three hours contemplating veins then trying to bring myself off under the covers in the hope that overt repetitive movement will tire me out. A relief like her eyes, Willow's, that say, 'Fine, phew,' and, 'Okay.'

And maybe, then, after splatting endorphins all over my stomach, or the pair of dirty boxers I usually take off and use as a mop, and after lying for fifteen more minutes with my limbs growing colder in the air growing bluer and the sheets even greyer and a finger fiddling in the splash of puddle, acting much like a curious child who hasn't seen something that strange before, or even tasted mud (just to see what it's like), feeling the void-like space in my arse left by the deflation of enlarged prostate stress, dry but a little crispy (will have to bathe for another three hours) after relentlessly tugging my doughy cock, underfilled, underpressurised, underused by someone other than you (me), until the final build to the depressing, pathetic and ultimately uninteresting crescendo, I'll fall asleep, and NOT dream of the *kukri* knife. The notch, the blade being pulled across the stranger's throat, catching blood in a Tupperware bowl. Surgical gloves. No, black cotton gloves, though they–

'Are you coming?' It's Willow, back from the toilet.

–could leave fibrous traces on the corpse.

'Coming?' I cough. It never happens. I barely sleep. I just lie there spilling out, spilling me, stroking and hoping the notch will catch my dribble, which comes thick and slow and dehydrated. Willow sits back down. Thin and underwired and possibly carrying someone's child, though by now it seems very unlikely. 'It's not knowing that scares me,' she says.

I say, 'Jesus, just take the fucking test.'

'But that's the thing,' says Willow. 'There's a part of me that enjoys being scared.'

'There's no way something's growing inside you,' I say. 'Now,' standing, 'if we keep sitting here we'll get shat on.'

Willow looks up at worriedly. 'I've been ready for ten minutes,' she says.

'Sorry, I was thinking.'

'What about?'

I put my hand in my jacket pocket and say, 'Nothing, cigarettes.'

two

Harry Gallon

CHAINSAW BALLET

'I want you to choke me with that belt.'
'What?'
'Choke me with the belt.'
'Still like it like that?'
'Don't laugh.'
'Sorry.'
'The belt.'
'What about it?'
'I want you to choke me with it.'
'Now?'
'Right FUCKING now. I want you to choke me with the belt. I want you to reach forward, while I'm pulling your hair, and take that black leather belt off the bed frame.'
'Wait,' she says. Bites my finger. Goes so tense I can feel the skin breaking between her teeth and then–
I let go of her ponytail and take my finger out of her mouth. Stop clenching my jaw. Pull out. Lie down. She turns around. There's a vodka cranberry on the bedside table. She climbs on top. She takes a sip, puts my dick back inside her and loops the belt round my neck.

*

The first thing she said to me when we met the night before was, 'Poison.' I'd arrived at the pub at 7:45. After coffee in the park she'd texted me and we'd agreed to meet at eight but I wanted to get there early. Neck a drink. Buy another and one for her then sit quietly at a table by a wall, with a view of the door. Except there was 'Poison,' behind me, while I stood at the bar.
'Willow?'
That's how she'd kill me.

'You're early,' I said.

She took a sip from a vodka cranberry and said, 'I wanted to get a quick drink at the bar, buy another (and one for you) then sit quietly at a table in a corner with a view of the door.' I sat down. Sniffed. There was a small thistle in a smaller, empty milk bottle between us. She moved it. 'Poison,' I said. 'I remember. I suppose a florist would know all kinds of things about naturally occurring toxins.' I eyed the pint she'd placed on the coaster in front of my chair, her hair a whole shade darker red lit up by the pound shop tea light. 'You've got half an hour,' she said, dipping her finger in the wax, 'to impress me. And if you make me laugh in that half hour,' picking wax off her finger, 'we'll ask for another candle.'

They're only supposed to burn for an hour, and that one was mostly gone.

I took a drink.

'What made you choose poison, anyway?' I asked her.

She shrugged.

'The thought of sitting opposite someone at dinner. Someone I had once known but no longer wanted to. The thought of watching them realise they were about to die. That it was already too late. And that there's no sense in a struggle.'

A pause.

'Are you hungry?' she asked.

'No,' I said, and she smiled a little. 'Wouldn't mind a cigarette though. Do you want to go outside?'

'It's a bit cold.'

'Have you got a filter?'

'Let me roll one for you.' She took some tobacco out of a tote bag on the floor, put a filter between her lips while she pulled out a paper, leaving a little bit of lipstick on the end.

'It might kill you,' she said, passing me the cigarette then starting again.

'Cancer,' I said, 'or your poisoned lipstick?'
'Ha!'
'Another candle, then?'
'It's not burnt out yet. But I could do with another drink.'
'Already?'
'Already. Is that bartender you know on tonight?'
'I don't think she ever leaves,' I said. 'Come on, I'll meet you outside.'

*

When I wake up Willow's standing by the bedroom window smoking a cigarette. There's a half-empty glass on the bedside table. It's not my bedside table. I cough. She says, 'So,' without turning round. 'So,' blowing smoke out the window (only open a little), 'So-o-o-o,' out of her mouth, into the draught and, like the smoke from the incense burning on the windowsill and drifting slowly outside, 'So, you're not dead, then.'

I cough again, take a sip from last night's drink, thinly veiled with a layer of dust, feel a slight crack in the centre of my bottom lip threatening to split open again. 'How did I do this?'

'I hit you,' says Willow. 'You passed out and I hit you.' She takes a drag. 'We shouldn't have done that.'

'I'm not wearing a condom. Did you–'

'No.' She takes another drag. 'When was the last time you were checked?'

'Um.'

'Well go then.'

'Right now?'

She raises her eyebrows. 'I'll have to go get a pill, anyway, for fuck sake.'

'What's that noise?'

'Come have a look,' she says, still standing by the window in a t-shirt, bare feet, small Persian carpet by a chair and a desk that looks unused, except for an empty bottle of wine. Outside, three men are attacking a tree. 'They've been doing it for hours,' she says. 'It's almost beautiful, I suppose.' One of the men is jumping between the branches on a line attached to a harness hooked up to the top of the trunk. 'See how his chainsaw dangles by his feet? He just swings about then whips it up when he needs it.' It's a small chainsaw, thirteen inch bar. He uses it with one hand. A second man, looking up, stands below in the neighbour's garden. When a branch falls to the ground he picks it up and chucks it over the fence to a third man operating a wood chipper in the street. 'This is the last tree,' says Willow. 'They did the other two while you were still asleep.'

She puts her fag out on the windowsill. There's a callus on her middle finger. It's orange, from too much smoking. Stabbing out. Incense uselessly drifts out the window. I cough.

She says, 'How'd you sleep?'

'Fine. Had a weird dream.'

'What happened?'

'I got hanged.'

'What for?'

'I don't know.'

She rolls her eyes, tries not to smile, asks me, 'Did you die?' but I lie and say I can't remember. 'If you die in a dream you die in real life,' says Willow. She walks over to the bed and sits back down, chainsaw in head and planes to Stansted and City airports with vapour trails outside. 'How about you, anyway?' I ask, sucking my swollen finger.

'Badly,' says Willow. 'We shouldn't have done that.' She rolls another cigarette. Willow's fingers are blood red and when she's rolled it she lights it and tries to take a drag from it but I kiss her. Quickly. Her lips are cold. I feel their moisture on the wind through the open window. She smiles like she doesn't know if she should, then says, 'It's disappointing of you.'

'That I passed out?'

'No,' she says, 'not the sex. When I asked you how you'd kill someone.'

'I chose a gun.'

'Yes. It's just so like a man.'

DISLODGED HUBCAPS

I can feel myself growing fatter. My muscles relaxing. Dissolving in bath water. Scrotum melting and spreading out like oil slick. Leg hair dancing. Toes grasping for the hot tap because I've been convalescing for roughly an hour. Keep meaning to climb out, dry off, go for a walk in the warmer air. But my towel's all the way over there, hanging on the hook on the back of the door. Keep feeling my testicles for lumps. And what's the point in making lunch? I've only been planning it all morning. I've got the shopping list my sister made for me. It just says cornflakes. And I've already missed breakfast. But sugar is bad for you and my thighs are chafing and I've got flat feet. Couldn't join the army if I wanted to and anyway I've already brushed my teeth. The bubbles are blue and float around my pubic hair, popping pop pop POP when I clench to pump blood into my dick, make it feel bigger as it emerges from the waterline, which is lowering because the plug has a crack in it.

My neck is itchy.

Earlier this morning, Willow sat staring at the portrait of young Stalin on her bedroom wall above the unused desk and dirty, neglected underwear which melted onto the floor. After giving her some money for the pill I left her at the pharmacy and walked three miles back to my house. It wasn't easy. Leg's barely healed. Can't cross roads that quickly. Drivers impatient. Dislodged hubcaps make me nervous. People driving around unaware that the sides of their wheels are jutting out like bone, snapped, to detach then lie there and litter the edge of the road. My head's killing me. My heart was beating and hasn't stopped since I walked back through my own door, locked it, lay in the bath still in my clothes and waited for it to fill up.

Real itchy.

A train leaves the station on the other side of the common. My bubble bath pops, the water level slowly decreases and I try to shrink myself and go with it as the sound of the train fades away and I think about my brother sitting at the side of the railway tracks at one end of the viaduct by our parents' old house, near the gravel pits which we dug out to hide ourselves in.

He was clutching a tuft of grass.

'The air can pull you back in,' he said. 'It's the same with water. That's why you should never jump off the side of a ship.'

'Why would you jump off the side of a ship?' I asked, from inside a derelict pillbox.

'If you were trying to kill yourself,' he said.

'Why would I want to kill myself?' I said, poking my head through a small hole in the concrete. My brother sighed. 'Maybe,' he said, letting go of the grass, 'someone was already trying to kill you, and you didn't want to give them the satisfaction.'

'Is it safe to come out yet?' one leg out of the pillbox door.

'Yes,' said my brother. 'The next train won't be along for another half hour.' He paused. 'Are you coming out of there or what?' He stood up, looking very adult, and I walked out through the low concrete door with my stick for a gun and followed him along the tracks and onto the bridge. When we were in the middle he turned round and said, 'You can see our house from here,' then pointed up through the valley.

He was carrying an old guitar amp.

'Are you ready?' he said.

I managed to take my phone out of my pocket before I got in the bath. It's resting on the radiator. Keeps lighting up. Missed calls from my father. Texts from my mother. My stomach grumbles.

Cornflakes.

I twist the cold tap with my toes and throw a stream of fresh milk into the bowl. Stops me sweating. Stops me obsessing about cancerous testicles and nosebleeds and why it stings when I piss and how many hairs can I count on my chest? Not many. When I got in the bath, after walking the three-or-so miles between Willow's flat and mine, I lay patiently and waited for my head to be submerged. Four minutes of listening to the vibrations of departing trains from the station across the common bore their way into the foundations of this block building and into my bathwater. Tiny bubbles of conversation dislodging from armpits and ear canals with a slight tickle, extreme desire to retract foreskin and clean under but, yes, the trousers. Arsehole, too, and toe jam consolidated by shoes, which might be ruined. Things that keep you normal. Text messages from Mother. Missed calls from Father. I held my breath, horizontal, for as long as was possible (thirty seconds, smoker), listening to the occupant of the flat below me practice a DJ set, or hang pictures of family members not yet dead, or fuck someone very loudly, with a quarter-inch jack plugged in up his backside and attached to a submerged, reverberating guitar amp pointed directly upwards, possibly even attached to the ceiling below my feet, with which I keep turning the taps to counteract the broken plug.

I'm listening.

'Throw it,' said my not-yet-dead-but-possibly-soon-because-the-next-train-was-due brother, who'd handed me his own crappy old guitar amplifier. We were standing on the viaduct, overlooking the watercress beds, the old abandoned concrete reservoir partially hidden by elder trees, a minute grey speck at the top of the big field behind our house and not that far from the barn we destroyed, our house there too, chimney coughing afterschool 60s Parkray what-to-dos into back-from-work arguments of WHERE ARE THE BOYS?

It was a school night.

'This amp's shite, anyway,' said my brother, referring to the 10 watt chipboard box he'd got at the discount shop in town, because he just wanted something good to smash, and had made me carry most of the way through the field to the gravel pit, to the holes we'd dug to commit our fantasy war crimes in, across the barbed wire enclosure by the watercress beds (private property) and the streams and meandering tributaries depositing forlorn winter fish in oxygen-free lagoons when the main river (it happened each year) gave up and waltzed to the sea.

'Are you ready?'

There was a hum.

'Is that the train coming?'

Clearly one of us had discounted the other rails, those that carry trains towards London.

I said to my brother urgently, 'Let's go.'

There was only a metre or so gap between where we were standing and the tracks that were carrying the approaching train. My brother said, 'No.' My brother said, 'Not until you drop it.'

'Why me?'

'Because it'll be good for you,' he said, as I leant over the brick kiln edge and let go.

Thirty seconds.

The guitar amp didn't really smash when it crashed into the stream that ran from the disused, discarded, outsmarted sluice gates at the opposite end of the watercress beds. It didn't really splash, either. It just sort of flopped, after falling in drunken slow motion, a sort of afterschool delirium, into the chalk riverbed. And sat, partially submerged, taking on water amongst the remnants of an old perambulator, some bottles of beer and a fridge-freezer that probably hadn't been hauled all the way up here, just lazily dumped underneath.

As the bath refills I sink my head without a sound. Without a BOOM travelling through the water except for gunshot pallets dropped CRACK banging on the concrete in the building site behind my flat. The gravelly drawl of the extractor fan tampering with leaves that've fallen through the wire mesh on the roof, somehow, and got caught in the belly button fluff fan-mechanism. A useless sluice gate pulled out by a discontented farmer as he dredges the part of the river that runs through his land, council on his back to flush all the crap downstream.

I believe I killed Gentleman Jim when I heard, as a child, that my mother, God bless her, once had an affair with him.

Just a thought.

The sound of the guitar amp slapping the shallow stream temporarily drowned out the hum from the railway tracks as the fast train (only three stops) approached the viaduct. When we were back on the earth embankment we held onto large tufts of wild grass by the abandoned pillbox. 'To stop the suction,' my brother yelled as the train passed feverishly, trying to ravage us, trying to untangle us, trying to end our misery. When it was over my brother re-righted his hair, scrunched his face and stood up. 'It's a very selfish thing to do,' he continued, 'standing at the side of a train track. The drivers get all kinds of mental issues, even if they miss you.'

I was standing in front of a tree, pissing.

'Good fun, though.'

My brother, feeling as alive as a crash survivor, said, as he began to crab-step down the side of the embankment back to the stream where the guitar amp lay collecting duck weed, 'Just remember: it can be a noble thing, standing at the side of a railway line, especially if you get hit.'

'Why?' I asked.

'Because,' he said, shaking his head, 'the train driver can claim medical leave,' twirling his fingers by the side of his ear.

'Does the same go for the drivers of boats?' I asked.

'The drivers of boats are called captains. Or maybe they're helmsmen. And no.'

'Why?'

'Because people can't walk on water.'

On the way home, after we'd traversed the poplars at the edge of the watercress beds and jumped over the holes we'd dug in the gravel pits and climbed the stile over the footbridge by the concrete housing for the unhoused, rusting sluice gates and crossed the field and reached the road, I made sure to step on every loose paving stone, see-sawing, just in case there was water beneath them.

The bathwater begins to get higher. I take a deep breath. This time I'm counting to forty.

MOTORBIKE RESCUE

The first time I heard my sister speak I was lying in bed in the dark. My brother was staying the night at a friend's house and I'd been put to bed early while my parents ordered curry, got tipsy on cheap chardonnay in a way to make their secretive, whispered, obligatory sex my gun oil wreck of a father administered agreeable. Bedroom door closed to the sound of, 'Be quiet.' And, drunk, 'Don't raise your eyes at me,' with a timid, 'Could you just slow down a bit?' in response.

I'd grown out of checking for house fires ever since I'd found my dead little sister reanimated beneath the sink by the toilet under the boiler in the bathroom. With wax for eyes, that refracted light like my grandfather's crystal whisky glass hidden behind a curtain while Mother the hoover sucked back up the mess of placenta and blood, as though she saw it too. Door closed, butter knife blade of light, heavy weight on my feet, like Father sneaking in on Christmas Eve, drunk and mince pied, buttery air under eye, over tired, and left stockings he felt ashamed for not being able to fill up.

The first thing my sister said to me was this: 'I taste like car keys.' It was dark and I'd only noticed the weight on my legs when it'd began to creep up from my feet, then, 'Keys. If you suck them, they taste like blood,' and I knew it was her. She smelled like our mother. Like post traumatic stress disorder. Like a birth that resembled, at least to my imagination, an unsatisfying defecation.

'It's the iron,' she said.

'What do you want?' I asked her.'

'It's good to finally meet you, too,' she said.

I was lying on my back. Her weight was pressing on my bladder, having crawled up my body and grown many years older since I found her, during an interval, crying quietly on the cold tiled floor beneath the sink near the boiler by the toilet in the bathroom downstairs. Pressing out the piss I was desperately trying to hold in but couldn't. I'd ruined my tolerance for dehydration. Would shrivel to lichen on a gravestone. All those alarm clock fire watch intervals late at night. Wake up, sit up, get up and check the house isn't burning down–

Silly boy.

–though really, I realised then, as my sister applied all her pressure until I gave in, closed my eyes and pissed myself, that I should've just started the fire.

*

I am alive because of Gentleman Jim. My mother was stranded at the side of a road with her bicycle. It had a puncture, or a rounded crank shaft, and couldn't be pedalled any further. Jim was out on his motorbike. It was hot. It was a sunny day. The air smelled like rape and hay fever.

I know this because she told me.

My sister.

My parents never actually elaborated. My father didn't know it. And my mother had tried to forget about it altogether.

'She loved him,' said my sister in the dark. I'd assumed she meant my father, to whom Jim had introduced her at the pub after stopping by the side of the road and offering to give her a ride.

'They hid her bike in a bush,' said my sister. 'I know this because I can see it. Turn on the light and you'll see it too.' But I was soaked through and clasped by the gold moons and stars that were printed on my duvet. 'I don't want to see you,' I said to her, feeling itchy and uncomfortably warm. 'Too late,' said my sister, who felt fully grown while she straddled me. 'The bubble has blown.'

Pop.

'You blew it up with that first shot.'

Bang.

'Though, let's be honest, who could miss a vertical rabbit at thirty yards with a shotgun? BLAM,' she shouted, slapping my chest with a much larger hand then I'd expected, before shrinking.

Loved him?

'Loved who?' I asked.

'Loved Jim,' she said. 'Rode his motorbike with him, with her arms around him on the back of his seat. She'd only been in the area visiting relatives. What else could've made her stay forever?'

She pulled the covers off and looked down at me.

'Naught boy,' flicking the wet waistband of my pyjama trousers. 'Don't worry, I'm here now,' she said, becoming a child again, less weight on my chest pushing down, breathing, pushing down, 'to tell you how you will die.'

THE NEXT TIME I WENT OUT SHOOTING

The next time I went out shooting with my father I pulled the head off a wood pigeon.

Snap.

Its bones didn't so much as crack as sort of just tear. Skin mottled under feathers jostled by my pubescent, bloody fingers, inexperienced but determined to prove that I could do other things besides piss the bed. A cute trickle of blood courted its beak while its eyes bulged in terror and anticipation. It was only a little thing. But then, so was I. My shotgun, smaller size, still managed to shoot this pigeon out of the sky as it tried to come in to land amongst the decoys my father had set out, after perusing his shooting textbook for twenty minutes.

'We won't throw it in the bag,' my father told me. 'We'll keep it out there, ready.'

'Why?' I asked him.

'To lure others in,' he said. 'We'll hold him up in the cradle.'

"The first time I held you, when you were born,
you were perfect: so sweet and so pure."

'But, you see,' said my father, not quite the same colour as a tree, 'You've not quite killed it.' The bird was flopping around in the stubble. 'Do you think it's a boy or a girl?' I asked.

'Doesn't matter, just grab it.'

I climbed out of the hide we'd spent the last hour constructing in the far northern hedgerow of one of the fields behind our house, about two-and-a-half miles from the barn my brother and I had burned down. 'Wait,' said my father, double barrelled, pointing to my .410 while I was halfway out of the entrance, 'break that first, young man.'

So I broke it, passed it to him, walked out into the field, which we chose because it had been recently harvested, twenty yards, feeling naked without the gun and wondering if my brother was watching me from somewhere through a telescopic sight.

'When you kill a pheasant this way,' said my father, 'it's quicker to grab it round the neck, just below the head, with your thumb and your forefinger touching, then spin the body round sharply. Its own weight will snap the necessary vertebrae in its neck. Much like that rabbit you killed the other day.'

'Okay.'

'Except a pigeon is much smaller. Put your hands together around its neck so that they're touching, then twist as you pull them apart.' This only seemed to strangle the bird, slowly. Its eyes bulged garishly, blood rejecting the beak and escaping to the ground. When the head came off my father said, 'Well,' in a shrugging sort of way. 'Don't worry about that.' Then he took the corpse from me, attaching it to the cradle (head included, though strangely inclined). After breaking his own gun and passing it to me, he climbed out of the hide, walked twenty yards back into the field and placed the cradle in the decoy formation we'd already laid down. The cradle had a long string attached to it which, when pulled from a distance, flapped the bird's wings for it.

'That should bring more in,' said my father.

PERAMBULATORS

Willow pours coffee from a large cafetière in her garden. There are five cubes of feta cheese on the green plate by the back door. 'Have you got any sugar?' I ask.

'You take sugar now?'

'How about milk?'

'Might be some in the fridge. Do you want any food?'

'I'm not hungry,' I tell her, standing by the trellis while a cat tightrope walks across some wire that holds up a dead grapevine. 'I just feel bloated, so I've been trying to walk a bit more. Leg's still sore, though.'

'Well, you did break it,' she says. 'How much longer are you signed off from work?'

'I got it extended.'

She nods, unhappily.

'Well, go easy,' she says. 'You don't want to hurt it again.'

'I don't see what difference it would make. I don't want to go back to work anyway.'

'They're paying you while you're off, right?' she says. 'It was only a broken leg. You'll be walking properly on it again pretty soon. Are you going to those therapy sessions?'

I don't think she believes what she's saying. Willow starts her day with The Guardian app. She sits on the toilet and reads the news. She sits on the toilet and hopes that something grey and lifeless plops out of her into the piss water.

'I read an interesting article the other day' she says, while I pour milk into my coffee. It turns solid, looks like lava. 'It was about a man who had extreme anxiety and paranoia.'

'Your milk's off,' I tell her, pouring my coffee away.

'He spent his whole life convinced that he was going to do something terrible. Is black okay?'

'Sure.'

The cat's eating feta cheese, loudly. Apparently he won't eat anything else, now.

'You should see his crap,' says Willow. 'Anyway, he spent all his time signed off from work because he had extreme anxiety and paranoia, and possibly some schizophrenia too because there was this part of him that knew he was going to kill someone, and part of him that wanted to. He said it started off small, worrying he'd accidentally spill a drink over somebody in a pub. Then it grew and he knew it wasn't about accidents, it was about potential. Rape somebody. Castrate somebody. Post nude photos of somebody on the internet. Push a buggy into a canal.'

'So what?'

'He couldn't sleep.'

'Let me guess,' I say, 'a strange figure standing by the edge of his bed with–'

'Yes.'

'–hands pressing down on his chest?'

'So you've read it too?' she says.

Is he terrified of himself? Does his fear cripple him? Sofa paralysis. Lying prostrate for days. Heavy breathing in strictly regulated bags. Inhalers with large volume spacers that look like penis enlargement pumps and only increase his anxiety. An old friend tries to take him out on late morning walks, but he feels too conspicuous and the attempts are destroyed by the presence of children on swing sets and micro scooters. Police sirens in the distance seem to be waiting for him. Always were. Families dragging dogs. Dogs dragging sticks. Mothers pushing perambulators along tow paths are easy targets. An accidental nudge and the baby has had it.

'Have you heard from Stephanie?' says Willow.

'No.' Pausing. 'She hates me.'

'No she doesn't.'

'She'll tell their children to avoid me.'

'No she won't.'

'It'll be like I never existed.'

'You're not listening,' says Willow.

'Sorry.'

She sips a little coffee. 'You should call her,' she says. 'She's family, remember?'

I cough.

Does he wake up in a sweat, having pissed himself? Does he lie the rest of the night awake, convinced that his body is rejecting him? Guts are black. Legs are broken. And if he cuts himself open his entrails won't be red, dark red and yellow fat of cholesterol, colon brown, and bone white.

No.

They'll be crude oil black. Immediate oxidisation. Instant rot. Colours changing behind his eyes. Instant death, much like when a doctor tells a middle-aged man he's got a terminal illness; that it has to be removed if he wants to live longer than two months more, and even then the odds aren't great. But if he hadn't booked the appointment, if he hadn't gone at all, he'd simply have a cough, or strangely enlarged testicles. Would've lived to become one of those ninety-two-year-olds who smokes and drinks and eats red meat and doesn't recycle.

'And your parents?' says Willow. 'Have you called either of them?'

'This garden's a mess, Willow.'

She rolls a cigarette. 'It's important to separate work and home,' she says, touching the grapevine, shrugging off a flowerbed. 'Well, at least you've got your sister.'

'Very funny.'

'Was she at the bar the other night?'

This joke's been going on for too long. It's too late to explain. And anyway, Willow wouldn't understand that when I asked her to choke me with that belt, that as I got close to passing out, close to coming, it was my sister riding me, not her. Hands on her waist. White knuckles. Up and down. Willow looking a lot like how my sister might look if I hadn't accidentally killed her.

'Close your eyes, brother.'

Alive.

'Close your eyes.'

Pulling the belt tighter as I let go inside of her.

Just a joke, right? Just that guy you met at university, who got pissed and told that story about a twin sister who died before infancy. Not your fault. Ghosts aren't real. Good round the dinner table, though. Good with some coke and discussing how to save the world at 4am. I knew her then, didn't believe it much myself. Can't deny it now, though. She knows me: 'You've a history of hurting others. Remember,' said my dead little sister as she choked me, spoke dirty, 'when you killed me?' It was her that night. Putting pressure and pressure on until I almost died.

Willow doesn't know about the Five Second Game. I'm too scared to tell her. And too scared to tell my brother's wife, still alive, raising their child, soon to be children, alone.

'What did he do,' I ask, 'the man in this article?'

Willow flicks her cigarette into an empty terracotta pot. 'He got over it,' she says. 'He spoke to doctors. He got on meds. He quit his job and left.'

'Left what?'

'Everything,' she says.

'And that worked?'

'He wrote the article, didn't he?'

I finish my coffee.
'I just don't think I deserve to be happy, Willow.'
She raises her eyes impatiently. The cat throws up.

RENDEZVOUS

I was watching Jim from the corner of the bar, surreptitiously sipping a half lager shandy while my brother and his friends looked around sheepishly, fake Ids ready in the event of any challenge. I was watching Gentleman Jim walk in, sit down and wait.

And wait.

I was watching him, Uncle Jim, meet a client.

This was all a coincidence. We'd accidentally walked into the hitman's date. Luckily, he hadn't seen us. And my brother was so far oblivious. He was sitting opposite me, facing towards the window and unable to see our uncle, Jim, sipping from a long tall drink, purple tie, hair slicked, and those same thin black gloves we'd seen him hold that stranger's head in, waist height, through the telescopic sight on that .243 rifle, that night under our pillows.

Jim had trimmed his moustache.

And I was kicking the table leg. Aiming for my brother's ankle but missing and hitting my dead little sister in her dead little head, beneath the table where she, never born (properly, at least), was hiding. Underage. Non-uniform day. One split lip from a punch by some kid I pushed over. Greasy quiff and peanut tie outside the maths block, fracturing the sympathies of my brother who, after wading in, told me that I deserved it.

'You'll always get it eventually,' said our dead little sister, not long from the nursery, which backed on to the primary school by the side entrance to our secondary.

'You told me to push him,' I said.

'I know,' she said, laughing. 'And you fell for it. What'd that boy even do to you?'

'He made fun of my trainers.'
'Well, they are pretty old. Look, they've got holes.'

'Come on then,' said my brother, who'd waited for me at the gates as usual, while his friends loitered outside the petrol station across the road. 'We're going down the road, try to sneak some beers. You can come if you shut up.' The pub we went to was known for not requesting ID but they still sat me behind a pillar so I couldn't be seen from the bar. 'Look who's there,' said my sister, hiding under the table. Uncle Jim had walked in a few moments later. 'He's looking very smart,' she said. 'Maybe I'll go hang out with his shoes instead of with yours,' poking my exposed toe. 'You're just a boy, after all,' squeezing my thigh. 'Plus, given his dangerous profession he's probably likely to die soon. Then we can both sit at your feet, although I,' she said, with the cheese Wotsit breath of a child, 'know better places to tease you.'

'What the fuck was that for?' said my brother, after I'd tried to kick my sister, missed and hit him. 'Look who's here,' I whispered, nodding towards Gentleman Jim and the long tall glass of what looked like vodka and cranberry in front of him. 'Must be a secret meeting.' My brother laughed, though not in a collaborative way. 'A covert rendezvous,' he said, shaking his head taking a drink. 'He must've got here early,' I said, checking the clock, 'on purpose, to get a good table with a view of the door. To scope out the floor. Keep a hand on the gun in his pocket, in case the meeting goes wrong.'

'Or well,' said my brother, smartly, before turning back to his friends.

My little sister, on hands and knees, was slithering over the floor in long socks and pleats to Jim's table, under which she crawled, sat cross-legged and winked at me. Meanwhile, another man, a stranger I didn't recognise, had entered the pub. He approached the bar and asked for a glass of water.

This was it.

Gentleman Jim hadn't seen him yet. He was drinking his drink and sniffing the menu. When the stranger approached him he put his hand on Jim's shoulder, quickly, before sitting down. 'Can I have another?' I asked my brother, who was drinking cider but who'd only allow me the one because, 'We're already pushing our luck here.'

My sister was listening to Jim's conversation. I peered round from behind the pillar again and saw Jim take his black gloves off the table top and put them into his coat pocket.

It was a black coat.

They were both very shady.

Just as you'd expect men to be when they're dealing in oral contracts.

If I'd been older I'd have gone round the corner and watched them through the window from under a fedora and waited until they left. I'd have followed them, expecting to find them in some warehouse or other, if they were working together, choking mercilessly some doomed enemy. Hands and knees. Repeating the name. Maybe a belt round the neck. A black leather belt. Gets on his knees as Gentleman Jim frees the belt from his trousers. Smacks him around. I'd be watching all this through the window, a spy, trying not to slip off the bin, watching, stroking the gun I'd been hoping I wouldn't have to use. An .08 Luger, or Browning high-powered pistol.

Double tap.

A leather strap around the neck.

My sister, who'd already suffered death by rotisserie umbilical cord, flopping around beneath the table, had infiltrated the meeting on my behalf because I couldn't be seen by my father's brother, and he, by the looks of things, didn't want to be seen by anyone.

The menu was clearly a ruse. A way for Jim to look true in his position as possible friend while this strange man sat opposite him without taking off his suit jacket, only occasionally sipped his water and talked an awful lot. Talked an awful, awful lot.

Reached across–

I was bent round the pillar.

–and took Jim's hand.

'Well,' I said to my sister later that night, after everyone involved had left to either dream about teenage sex or commit murder before going to bed. 'Well,' after lying to my mother about my swollen lip–

"You don't have to play contact sports if you don't want to, love."

–and after lying to my father about my swollen lip. 'Well,' to my sister, who was lying underneath my cabin bed on the futon I used to play PlayStation on instead of studying Roosevelt's New Deal or algebra. 'Well, I didn't expect Jim to tell him that his time was up in public. Do you know what he said?' I asked her. 'Did you hear what Jim said to the stranger? Why he wouldn't stop talking? Why he looked so sad and scared and took Jim's hand and pleaded?'

'He just said he was sorry.'

'What?'

'He just kept saying honey, honey, honey.'

Over.

And.

Over.

'Honey?'

'I think it was a nervous twitch,' she said. 'Probably saw it on the menu Jim was holding in front of him. Saw honey-glazed ham. Honey-roasted vegetables. Milk and honey. Honey and whisky. Probably got stuck in his doomed head. Prob–'

'Makes sense,' I said, two feet from the roof while my brother was asleep on the other side of the room. Just then a loud creak. Footsteps on the ladder, approaching the ceiling.

'Keep it down.'

'When are you going to ask them to get rid of this thing?' said my sister, climbing on. 'You're not much of a child, are you. How many children do you know who have committed murder?'

'Fuck you.'

She was sitting by my feet.

'Take your hands out of your pants,' she said.

'Not very manly, is it? All that begging. And in such a public, um, position. Probably why the guy who'd hired Jim in the first place wanted the stranger dead. You can't have weaklings in that line of work.'

'It wasn't the same stranger as the stranger we saw before, was it?'

'How could it have been?'

'They looked awfully similar.'

'But you only saw the back of one's head. No, he's dead. These kinds of men go from one job to another like that.'

Click.

'He must've given something away,' she said. 'Something important. To the police, or a rival gang.'

Pause.

'Where do you think Jim did it?' I asked.

'Did what?' she asked.

'Killed him,' I said.

'I saw them by the door to the kitchen,' she said. 'I think maybe Jim strangled him there.'

'Go to fucking sleep,' said my brother.

PLATE LICKERS

What happened next was, and remains, confidential. It was the middle of the night and I was woken by the sound of weeping. Before my not-yet-dead brother had gone to sleep, while my dead little sister and I were doing our teeth in the bathroom downstairs, over the sink by the boiler next to the toilet where I'd first found her, feet tiptoeing across the floor in the cold where, years before, she lay in a puddle of broken water and blood, we'd (at her suggestion) drunk several bladder-full glasses of water.

We needed an interval. Just one.

The door to our bedroom was closed when I heard the weeping. It was a snotty kind of weeping. A wet fart kind of sobbing. An all-hope-is-lost kind of pleading for the chance to live again.

Gentleman Jim.

Who, we soon discovered, was once again holding a stranger's head.

And we really did see this through a window.

Holding a head at the back of a neck, knuckles white, gasping.

'Looks like quite a struggle,' she'd said. My sister. Twisting her ponytail between her fingers and biting her lip. 'That man, that stranger, really must want to stay alive.' It was the middle of the night and my brother was snoring a teenage snore, with one foot out of the duvet cover, and there was a thick green light on the floor, inviting me out to the hallway.

My sister wasn't with me. She'd left a note that said, 'Meet me at Jim's house,' which I knew was part of the plan and had already checked the tyre pressure on my mother's old Traffic Master, less traceable than my mountain bike, which I'd strategically placed by the back door before my parents turned out the lights.

'Bring protection.'

Jim lived in a small town six miles down the road from our village. He lived in a small flat above a row of shops with a black metal stairwell round the back that led up to the front door and the cold vinyl floor that he swept every day and, at the back, behind the utility room where we weren't allowed to go, the desk drawer with the lock.

'I'd heard Jim say it was over,' said my sister, who I'd met next to Jim's parked motorcycle by the first step, 'at the pub earlier. Jim kept saying to the stranger, "It's okay. It's okay. It's going to be okay." He said, "This is how it has to be."' And then she looked at me. 'Did you bring it?' I checked in my pockets but there was only my wallet which she took from my hand and emptied. 'Is this it?' she asked, holding a rotten fiver and a condom I'd taken from my brother's bedside drawer. 'I couldn't find the key to my father's gun cabinet,' I said.

She shook her head. 'Doesn't matter,' she said. 'Just follow my lead.' And she began gnawing on the motorbike's brake cables.

A light went on in the flat above the shops. We were crouching on the twelfth step, behind the bins where the kitchen window opened out. Jim was walking around his open plan kitchen with an apron on, wiping his hands and comprehending dishes in the sink which was spattered with red flecks and half-eaten sausages. 'He's been at it again,' said my sister, dead, as she twirled her hair.

The black gloves lay deflated on the arm of the sofa.

'He must've done the job here, then cut up the body in the utility closet that no one else is allowed to go in.'

Jim removed the apron. He'd gone from the kitchen into the study, which was at the back of the open-plan living room, to get a black duffel bag. When he came back he took a key from his pocket and stood in front of the door to the utility closet, which he then opened before he, half-standing inside, began filling the bag.

'Can you see what he's putting in there?' she asked.

I was hiding under the camouflage hat my father had got me for shooting. But Jim wasn't a pigeon. Jim was a fox. And foxes have good hearing.

I said, 'Shh.'

Jim had filled the bag. And Jim had changed his shirt. And Jim was turning off the lights to leave the flat but stopped to lick something red from a dirty plate by the sink.

Jim opened a drawer and took out some clingfilm.

Jim picked up one of the uneaten sausage pieces and wrapped it up.

He put the wrapped up sausage in his bag then took the black gloves off the arm of the sofa.

He turned off the light by the window, without closing it, and opened the door.

'What's more,' said my sister, sifting through Al Stewart records and dipping fingers in pools of red liquid round the sink while I looked through glass jars and bottles and key trays, 'is you've eaten dinner here before. Pretty gross.'

'There's a lot less blood than I thought there'd be,' I said from inside the bathroom.

'Do you know how much a man bleeds when you cut off his dick?' said my sister.

I said no.

She said, 'It's a giant vein, remember.'

By the sink.

'An artery.'

Checking dishes. 'Did you see him lick the blood off these?' she said holding plates. 'It's like the Titanic. Seal off the bulkheads but the blood keeps on spilling.'

'I thought he was already dead,' I said, from the corner by the door to the utility room. 'I thought you said he strangled him by the bins behind that pub?'

'Well,' she said. 'I did see them round the back of that kitchen.'

'Did you see Jim do it?'

'No. Jim would never be so public. He would've cut the man's throat with the *kukri* knife. He would've–'

'I know.'

'–pulled, yes pul-l-l-ed, slowly pulled the twelve inch blade across the stranger's jugular. Adam's apple. Voice box. His vocal cords would've snapped like guitar strings and reverberated with the gurgling of air and blood.'

'Kind of like when you have a snotty nose,' I said, at Jim's desk. 'So let's check.' I expected the drawer to be locked, so when I went to open it I used too much force and the whole thing fell out. 'Wait,' said my sister, whose hair had grown longer, 'let me.' And she pushed me aside abruptly.

'What do you see?' I asked. It was dark. We couldn't turn on the lights in case Jim came back after dumping the body parts.

'DVDs,' she said.

'What kind?'

She giggled but said, 'Never mind. The knife's gone.'

'He must've taken it with him.'

'Yes,' she said, closing the drawer. 'For protection.'

I checked my back pocket to make sure my wallet was there.

There was nothing in the utility closet. Just a washing machine, a tumble drier and a boiler set on heat. No sign of a struggle. No sign of bone marrow and no congealed blood.

Not even a pubic hair.

'Very thorough,' said my sister, dead, as we followed Jim to the address we'd found written down on the pub receipt he'd left by the landline. 'Do you think it's a b&b?'

'No chance. This is a small town. People won't tolerate covert operations at the best of times. These people are small-minded. Too curious. Nosey. And quick to reject anyone dissimilar to them.'

'Well, aren't we?'

'We're truth seekers,' she said in the darkness. 'We've got to find evidence. We've got to find proof so our brother believes us.'

'He's not you brother,' I said. 'He's mine.'

'So's the blame,' she said, sighing. It didn't matter, anyway. My brother no longer seemed necessary to convince. No longer lived in the forts we'd built, the bird hides, the telescopic sights. 'He's got bigger, more blood-filled things on his mind,' my sister said as we left Jim's flat.

The address led us a few streets over to a business hotel: red brick, faceless, the perfect place to meet a murder accomplice, or a crime syndicate boss. The kind of person with bodyguards and money-laundering schemes Gentleman Jim would probably work for.

'Around here?' I said. 'I doubt it.'

'You saw the man's penis, right?'

'I thought it was leftover sausage?'

'You saw the blood flecks on the dishes and the stained red apron? You saw Uncle Jim wiping his hands after the fact, finished with the act. Did you SEE those Beatles records?'

'I feel bad for slashing his motorbike tyres.'

'Well don't. That way he can't follow your bike tracks when you go back home.'

The receipt paper had ROOM 17 written on it in pencil.

Room 17 was on the first floor. My sister and I looked over from the same old churchyard with the yew tree in it. The same telescopic cemetery bushes with the same downhill view to that stranger's house, the first instance of catching Jim (almost) in the act, before our father's feet hit the stairs and echoed work in the morning.

'Look,' my sister said to me with an elbow. She elbowed me out of the corner of the hollow yew tree we were hiding in, only facing a different way. 'Stop fucking around and see.'

'What's this?'

'It's the telescopic sight from Jim's .243,' she said. 'There's no sense in wasting ammunition, so we can use it as a regular telescope. And besides, he's family.'

'I'm cold,' I said.

'Try being dead,' she said. 'Here,' passing me the rifle scope. 'Take this.'

'Don't you need it?'

'I've seen it all already.'

We were watching through the window of Room 17. Nice curtains. Purple bedspread. Gentleman Jim sitting on a cheap armchair next to a service tray. Milk pots and UHT creamers. A stained kettle and the remote control for an old TV. We couldn't see his feet or the black bag he'd filled with body parts.

Jim was waiting.

He'd got there early, to get a good chair and feel ready.

'What's he eating?' said my sister.

A sausage, half eaten. And some olives with feta cheese on a green plate. Jim was still wearing his black gloves and his eyes were fixed readily on the door. 'Seems amateur,' I said out loud, 'to be waiting for a mob boss by an open window. The curtains aren't even drawn. What if we had a rifle and a desire to kill? What if we were friends with the murdered strangers?'

'The one with the dog? Or the one whose dick he's eating?'

'Does it matter?'

Uncle Jim was sipping from a glass of water. He seemed pretty relaxed. He barely even moved when another man entered the room, and then another, younger, man after him.

'He's in handcuffs,' said my sister, with the younger man in her sights.

'Now they're hugging,' I said, though she'd already seen the second, older man, approach Jim, who'd risen from his chair, leaving his water (suspiciously amber in colour) by the green plate. 'Quite intimate, these gangsters,' said my sister. 'Blood ties, I suppose. But not the kind that pass down through procreation. I bet that when they let a new member into their, um, coven–'

'Their gang.'

'–they, yes, gang, when they let a new man in they have to cut their hands with a knife. Their right hands. Then they touch their wounds together.'

'I think a coven's just for women.'

'Well, they do bleed differently, I guess.'

'What do you mean?'

'Doesn't matter.'

In a puddle, under a sink next to a boiler by a toilet in a downstairs bathroom. Or on white cotton sheets in the middle of the night, expecting twins.

'He must be a prisoner,' said my sister, who felt older than me because she seemed to know everything. 'Darling,' she said, which was strange, 'I know everything that's going to happen in your life. You just have to trust me.'

I didn't.

But still I wanted to see.

I wanted to see what was going to happen.

I wanted to see the older man and Jim, my uncle, strip him.

The third man, who looked almost a boy.

'Can't be more than twenty-four,' she told me, and yet now he seems younger than I was then. 'Must be a snitch. Jim delivers the goods,' pointing at the older man who was looking into Jim's black duffel bag and smiling, good, sadistic, dead, dealt with that stranger now here's another, 'so the boss can get a look.'

'They all seem quite close,' I said. 'They all seem to know what's going to happen. What HAS to happen.'

'See that?'

'See what?'

'The younger man, the boy,' said my sister. 'They've removed his handcuffs and he's taking something out of the bag.'

'Is it another sausage? They're all very hungry, aren't they.'

'It's not a sausage,' she said, raising her eyes which had dilated into completely milk-white pupils that consumed her face. 'It's the *kukri* knife.'

The boy was holding it in front of him. His knuckles were white. It looked big in his hands.

'Remember that trick at school?' I said.

'I never went.'

'When you make a pencil bend by holding it at one end, loosely, between your index finger and thumb, then sort of shake it up and down. It looks like it's bending, but it's just an optical illusion.'

The boy was holding the blade, shaking it up and down.

'Uh huh,' said my sister, growing younger again. 'What's he doing now?'

'He's holding it in front of him like a twelve inch long–'

'He's smiling. And LAUGHING.'

'He must know that he's done wrong,' I said. 'To so happily go to his death.'

By now the younger man was on the bed. He'd been ordered to remove his clothes by the older man who was now waving the knife around casually, still wearing his suit and purple tie, looking veiny. Uncle Jim was rolling up a note and sniffing coke off the green plate. Of course, I didn't know this then. I just saw him unravel some rope then tie the younger man up. He tied his wrists and he tied his ankles. The rope was black. He'd pulled it from one of the pockets on the side of his bag. The younger man was on his back, looking nervous, rope round his body parts and rope round the back of the bed and down to the legs because it didn't have posts.

'They're going to cut his balls off,' said my sister, twirling her hair even more. 'They're going to cut his balls off and shove them down his throat.'

'But why would they do it in a ho–'

'Don't ask questions with obvious answers,' she said. But I didn't know what, exactly, she meant.

The older man was slowly dragging the blunt side of the *kukri* knife over the young man's groin. Gentleman Jim was fiddling with something in his pocket. I was sure it was a gun. Pillow for silencer. Just finish him off and be done with it, I thought. One shot (9mm) to the head and get out of it. I couldn't understand it. Everything was taking ages. The younger man looked too happy. As though they were actually helping him. As though the older man and Jim were preparing to remove a cancerous tumour from him. Removing great weight of pressure from him. Looked ready to burst from excitement. Twisted his wrists and ankles, bare, bald chested as I felt it. The rope. The rush of blood to the, nope, didn't know what that was (in a whisper, to my sister, who I'd jabbed with the front of the scope).

Or an elbow.

Or a, 'Stop stroking that.'

Pause.

'This isn't a fucking joke,' she'd said, poking me in the shoulder.

Get your hand out of my head.

Get you out of–
They were stroking the younger man's forehead.
–my head.
They were sweating.
Get you–
Stroking.
–out.

I didn't actually see them cut him open.

'Excuse me?'

'I was distracted. A fox howled, somewhere in the cemetery.'

'Do foxes howl?'

'Maybe. Somewhere at the bottom of the cemetery, near the house we'd spied Gentleman Jim in previously, dragging his long, hard knife across the throat of the stranger.'

'Which one? There've been so many. I don't remember.'

'At the bottom, by the war graves, surrounded by the trees. Near the gate which opens out onto the street with the psychiatric hospital.'

'A fox?'

'Yowling. Howling. Zipping across.'

Uncle Jim heard it, too. He paused what he was doing and looked out through the window towards our hollow yew tree. Snipers cover their rifles with cloth. Modern telescopic sights have slit-eye covers that fit across the front lens to prevent glare from the sun. In this case it was a child's hand. My hand whipped across and I ducked my head and said, 'He's seen us,' to my sister, but all of a sudden she was gone. The younger man, tied up, was licking coke residue off the plate as the older man, still in his suit, held it in front of his face. It can't be over yet, I thought.

Then Jim undid his top button and drew the curtains.

BIN CAKES

There are many differences between northern mockingbirds and Eurasian jays. The northern mockingbird has a call like a telephone bringing good news. The Eurasian jay has a call like a vacuum cleaner being wheeled round a house, its power cable slapping like tides against skirting boards on a landing, the electricity being turned on and off.

It was a Sunday. Gentleman Jim had come round for lunch. Lunch was roast beef. It'd been in the oven since nine in the morning. My mother had been in the kitchen, caramelising, since seven and my father had been reading papers or checking oils or thinking about sharpening his chisels and about cleaning out his steel tool box and about buying more two-stroke for the hedge trimmer, growing thinner in his brain and fatter in his chair. Listing to port in order to answer the telephone which rang while my brother was bang bang banging some old pieces of wood together outside, and I was upstairs under my cabin bed with my sister's corpse, barking like a dog in anticipation of Jim's arrival.

'I've invited Jim to lunch today,' said my mother to my father at breakfast, while my brother was shovelling overcooked bacon and my mother was coating chipolata sausages, out of, then back into, the oven. 'Uh huh,' said my father, an empty dressing gown.

'Want to help me bake a cake for pudding later?' my mother asked me. I didn't answer. I was busy watching my sister who was busy tormenting the terrier in the covered-up area where the chimney used to be. 'You can lick the bowl.'

'What kind of cake is it?' I asked her, just as Father emerged with a whistle and suggested, 'The usual, no doubt.'

'I think he's jealous,' my dead sister whispered to me. We'd gone understairs and were sitting under the cabin bed. 'I think he suspects that your mother and Jim had a love affair.'

'A what?'

'Or that they're having one right now.'

'I don't want to be of those kids with divorced parents,' I said, with my head round the socks I was putting on and downstairs the dog barking as the telephone began to ring. 'I wonder who you'll live with,' said my sister, unwilling to miss a chance to wind me up. 'Probably your father. I wouldn't blame mum if she just ran away with him.'

'With who?'

'With Jim.'

'What do you mean?'

'You never listen,' she said. 'Don't you appreciate all the information that I give you? Your uncle's a dangerous man. And a handsome one, too.'

'He's too old for you.'

'Age isn't a problem when you've never really been born. I was reabsorbed, remember? Reabsorbed by our mother, so therefore I live inside her. She didn't wipe me up with a dishcloth off the floor of the downstairs bathroom. I'm not a cum stain or shit stain or why-hasn't-it-happened period pain, like you fucking well are.'

She paused.

'What are you doing?' she asked.

I was turning on the PlayStation.

'You're getting fat,' said my sister, half hanging from the bed.

'I know what you're doing up there, young man,' my father shouted up the stairs. 'Wash your hands and come get in the car.'

'Where are we going?' I shouted.

'To pick up your uncle,' he yelled back. 'His motorbike isn't working.'

*

Northern mockingbirds are rarely, if ever, seen in Britain or continental Europe. Eurasian jays prefer north-west Africa to North America. It was a Sunday in Southern England and my father had finally diagnosed me insane.

What a relief.

We'd gone to pick up Uncle Jim from town. Broken bike. Car horn father. Mother couldn't imagine who'd do such a thing.

I was yawning. Dad was beeping.

'I can't express how grateful I am to have you guys around,' said Jim round the table, reaching out over half-empty serving dishes and taking my mother's hand. 'I don't know what's happening. It's a bit scary, actually. No one's ever done something like this before.' My father looked away and under the table my sister was whispering something so loud no one could hear it: 'Don't worry, he'll pin it on one of his enemies.'

She was kneeling. In knee-high white socks. Hair in a bob. Feeding our still-alive terrier scraps of cheap beef I'd had only a little trouble shifting from the eyes of my mother, who kept repeating, 'This is great.'

Back and forth.

'Isn't this wonderful?'

Fresh leeks from the garden and fresh plasters on her arm.

'He'll assume it was another assassin,' said my sister, teasing the terrier until it got bored and tried to sniff Jim's balls instead. My sister followed the dog. 'She can probably smell his last victim's DNA.'

'Stop looking at your lap, boy. Have some manners.'

'Sorry Dad,' I said.

My father turned back to Jim. 'Don't you think it could've been him?' he asked.

'I don't know. No, it can't have been. It was a very amicable breakup,' said Jim. 'We had a good, long chat in the pub.'

'Maybe he saw you with some other fella,' said my father. 'You do look like you had one hell of a night.'

'Oh, leave him alone,' said my mother. 'Do you want some cake?'

My sister was sitting between my mother and Jim, sucking a wooden spoon.

'What did you get up to last night, anyway?' asked my father.

'That's none of our business,' said my mother, nodding in my direction and in the direction of my still-alive brother, who was brooding.

Smiling, Jim said, 'I'd love some.'

My father raised his eyes.

Outside someone was hoovering. Near the fence that separates the back garden. In the pine trees. My father stood up and walked to the window. 'There's a bloody great jay in that tree,' he said, and in my brother's direction continued, 'quick, get your air rifle.'

My brother frowned, shook his head and helped himself to more bread sauce until my father stopped standing at the window and went into the cupboard underneath the stairs to get the .410. 'Go on then,' he said to me as he broke the gun and from the dressing table picked up a cartridge before passing both across the table. I looked towards my mother but she was nowhere to be seen.

'Where is she?' I asked my sister, who was pawing for a treat by Jim's legs. When my father had gone to the cupboard my mother had disappeared. 'Who cares,' said my sister, 'I bet you could really impress him,' meaning Jim, 'if you take that gun and with one shot plop that bird off its perch in the pine tree. Show him you're dangerous. Show him you can't be messed with.'

I walked outside very carefully. Our backdoor creaked heavily so I took a good thirty seconds just to open then close it behind me. Eurasian jays are good at mimicry. They can make you believe they're something else. This bird had stopped hoovering and was creaking down at me, suspicious. My sister had followed me outside and was hiding behind the remains of an old bicycle frame next to the broken greenhouse. My father was watching through the kitchen window, making sure I lifted the gun properly, stood properly, breathed properly.

'I know where your mother is,' my sister whispered to me. 'She's round the other side of the house with Uncle Jim.' I looked at the kitchen window. My father pointed at the tree. Jim was no longer sitting at the table. The jay kept creaking. I left the gun by the broken bike frame and walked to the front of the house. As I approached I heard sniffing. My mother and Jim were smoking cigarettes by the front door and there were tears in my mother's eyes, though she smiled when she saw me.

BANG.

My mother winced as she took a drag. 'Would you just give us a moment, little man?' said my uncle. I walked back round the corner of the house, where I stood, listening. 'It's relentless,' said my mother.

Drag.

'Just relentless.'

Drag.

'My food. My driving. The way I try to raise our children. You know he still wants to send them to public school? But with what money?'

'It'll be fine,' said Jim. 'He just wants what he thinks is best for them.'

For a while my mother said nothing. I'd slumped down at the side of the house, in the flowerbed with the discarded toy army men.

'It's the guns, too,' she said, after lighting another cigarette. 'This obsession with shooting. Even at the dinner table. He can't help but get up to kill something.'

'It's meant to be sporting,' said Jim.

'But a mockingbird?' said my mother. 'He makes our youngest son shoot a mockingbird?'

'It was a jay, dear,' said my father, who'd gone back into the house, through the dining room to the front hallway by the staircase and the front door, opened it and stepped outside. 'A Eurasian jay. Those two birds are not the same.'

I could hear her stamp out her cigarette on the concrete pathway.

'Smoking again, are we?' said my father, which sent my mother storming past me, still crouched in the flowerbed, half-hidden but never gotten rid of. She, Mother, stopped briefly, looked as though she was about to say something. Maybe she sensed the presence of her miscarried daughter. Certainly she saw me eavesdropping.

She kept walking.

That's when my sister appeared. She was holding the dead bird. 'It's very pretty,' she said. 'Look how blue it is.'

I said, 'Shh,' still trying to listen. My sister shrugged, dropped the bird and left.

'Why do you encourage her?' my father asked Jim round the corner.

'Smoking?' said Jim, who himself was lighting another.

'Not only that,' said my father. 'She's mothering these boys too much.'

'They're just close.'

'Too close, I think.'

'She said you want to send them to boarding school.'

'Oh, I don't know. It's only ever been a thought. It might do them good, like us. We turned out fine, didn't we?'

Drag.

'We only went there because our dad was an officer.'

'We went for a walk last weekend,' said my father. 'Her sister came round with her kids. The children took their bikes but he–'

Meaning me.

'–had a tantrum.'

'Why?'

'I don't know. I can't remember. Something about pushing his bike up a hill? That's right, it got a puncture. So he just dumped it in a hedge at the side of the road. He's meant to be a fucking man, but he's mad as anything.'

My uncle laughed. 'He's still a child,' he said, taking a drag. 'Has he heard the story about how you two got together?'

My father coughed in the smoke. 'No, he hasn't. Besides, her bike was actually broken. She needed help.'

'How old were you when you got married?' said Jim.

'It was different then,' said my father.

'Maybe,' said Jim. 'At least you're right about one thing: she really did have a good reason to drop her bike that day. In fact, I'm surprised it's the only thing she did drop, after she saw me on my motorbike.'

'Very funny.'

Just then my mother reappeared, holding a trowel. She picked up the dead bird and walked quickly, with purpose, round the side of the house to my father. 'Bury it,' she told him, holding out both of her hands.

My father said, 'Look, it's just a–'

'Bury it.'

I CAN HEAR MY MOTHER PRAYING

I've been repairing the entrails of my mother's old green bicycle ever since I killed my brother. There was nothing of him left to touch, let alone fix. His flesh was dr-dr-dripping from his skeleton while everyone else we knew was gathering for somebody else's funeral. It's funny, really. The old green bike's been chained to the railing on the concrete walkway outside the front door of my flat ever since it was given back to me by the fire brigade. Or the police. Or the forensics team. I don't know what any of them were searching for when they took it. It was a tool inadvertently used to introduce my parents, so maybe it was considered a murder weapon.

I want to burn everything down. I want to burn down that house and my house, but I can hear my mother whisper. She's saying please. Her words are WD-40 destroying rust. They didn't start with her old green bike flying through the air but that certainly amplifies them. Makes them echo through fat rolls whenever I squat to undo the de-rusted bolts.

I've been assessing potential fire escapes. The walkway on the sixth floor to which my front door leads looks out across a school playground. It'd be a hell of a spectacle to fall during school hours. I don't trust the elevator mechanism in this building. It's wide enough for cadavers.

I can hear her. She's miles away, with a new life in better weather. But whereas my father always chose to blame the universe for his misfortunes, she knew it was easier to rely upon it for answers. It took a long time for her to realise (and my father never did) that the reasons for most things are in the silence that answers you.

It's an eighty foot drop from the walkway. Not what I'd intended, really. And anyway, it'd be too easy to escape down the stairway. You don't take elevators during fiery situations, and I'm a coward. I already tried squeezing my foot into the rubbish shoot, but it barely takes a shopping bag full of used tissues and uneaten curry as it is.

I don't think the other mothers would ever forgive me if I set fire to a large family building 150 feet from their children's school.

I've built the pyre but my mother's been praying for rain.

There'd be no evidence for the police to obtain. Dust burnt.

New plan.

The school children are playing football. One of them drops from an abusive tackle and scrapes his knee on the tarmac. No dirt to dig into. And some of the older kids are lingering on the peripheries, passing fivers through the high metal fence to someone selling weed. Another stands with his hands in his pockets by the corner of one of the school buildings. Bunsen burners through the open windows as, head-down, he whistles when student teachers my age, carrying lanyards and litter-picking claw arms, get too close.

Her prayers are inside the chainring. Her prayers are squeaking. My mother's old green bicycle has needed oiling for a very long time, but now the rims are bent and some of the spokes are snapped. There's a significant dent in the crossbar. Load-bearing chain tension left lying on the side of the M1.

Or was it the M11?

I spend a lot of my time nowadays lying in bed smoking cigarettes, thinking about how quickly the place will catch fire if I move everything into the centre of each room and collect all the dust and fluff and pubic hair that's gathered by the skirting. I could turn everything I own and rent into a tinder box, then hit it with a high-velocity shot of deodorant can and lighter. Whole place would go up like a Sherman tank. And I could stand across the road, stand on the opposite pavement, and watch as everything I don't want goes up in smoke.

Her words are terrifying. They bring me back to that home with an urgency. Sent my brother and sister, Mother, Father and me to church ceremony. They lit candles for phantom babies and candles for dying marriages and candles for just because. Full circle. Last pew. Scrutinising neighbours. Hands on brown radiators. Father ringing the bells all by himself. No one we know actually believes this shit, but there's a desperate need to be part of something.

'It's no use,' I say to the railing outside, out loud, flicking my fag end down down down six floors and onto the pavement behind the school playground. 'I can't bang this dent out.'

My hammer's softer than the bike.

My parents almost didn't have us. They tried and tried, but nothing happened. Just before they conceived my brother, my father told my mother, 'It's better to have tried.' They gave up and bought the terrier. Then BOOM. My brother. BOOM, me. And boom, the dog would get hit by a car on the road outside our house many years later. My brother and I dug the grave while our mother prayed and our father checked the time, the dog's death an omen that reassured him he could at least blame the careless driver for ruining his marriage.

Getting the back wheel off is a chore. The rear mudguard is held on with oestrogen and a thick black cable tie which refuses to be cut with anything I have in my cardboard toolbox. Both tyres are flat, but the rubber didn't melt. The bike was thrown at least fifteen feet into a damp English hedgerow before everything caught on fire and exploded. The tyres are simply corroded. They're outdated. Old. The rims are rusted and the rust has stained the rubber orange. Brown, even. There's black gunk oozing out of the hub gear and the handlebar has been pinched inward, presumably by the impact.

It bounced several times.

My dead little sister says, 'You should chuck it over the edge.'

She's been watching me all morning through the kitchen window.

The school bell rings. A rusted bolt finally gives on the end of the crank shaft and the chainring catches my finger. My mother prays from the new flat she rents alone, watching out for tetanus. She wanted to be closer to Stephanie, to her grandchild and, soon, her dead son's new baby. More focused on hysterectomies. Left me just enough time to shout, 'Fuck,' loud enough for the kids hanging out by the high metal fence to hear, and look up, before being ordered into a line outside the science block.

Nearby, a church bell rings two o'clock.

BB GUN MASSACRE

Once, a tree fell down in our village and crushed a tree surgeon's apprentice.

SPLAT.

One of the controlling wires snapped.

CRACK.

When it snapped the tree fell the incorrect way, which also happened to be directly onto the corpse (née body) of a sixteen-year-old boy, still holding a saw.

It was a beech tree.

He'd been in my brother's class.

My father had a chainsaw, too. My brother and I used to go into the woods at the top of the field behind our house with him, to chop wood. He didn't stop aspiring to be detached from the rest of the village. They, after all, kept hiring the same tree surgeon to alter the aesthetics of their greens.

The woods my father used to chop in were behind the field with the old abandoned concrete reservoir in it. There was a new reservoir, somewhere. It was metal, shiny. My brother found it one day, while our father was chainsawing the remains of a beech that had fallen in high winds. I'd climbed up another tree, and couldn't get back down. I yelled, but no one could hear me.

*

The soundtrack is: a scarecrow banger thrown onto a village hall dance floor during the annual flower show, disrupting a hokey cokey.

No.

Police sirens. Testing the response time of the London Metropolitan Police Service (I always wanted to test the response time of the London Metropolitan Police Service). Always wanted to test the response time of my nerves. It started with the Five Second Game (part one), when I held the playground end of that .410 shotgun under my chin. Loaded.

The sound track is: click. Or the soundtrack is a little boy stuck up a tree. Or maybe the soundtrack is, actually, one of my grandfather's dead, rusted shotgun cartridges, requisitioned from the old understairs gun cabinet (next to the door for the downstairs bathroom), redistributed into an angry old farmer's barn.

That's a fizz.

A fizz from my brother, who laughed popping candy laughter like tin and pebbles. Or a cheap guitar amp meddling with the course of a stream's water. Or the sound of reams of paper being torn by his younger brother–

Me.

–every time he (I) tries (try) to write a sorry letter ('I'm sorry') to his widowed wife ('for killing my brother') for killing her husband, the love of her ('and ruining your') life.

*

For a while it was The Mike Curb Congregation and their song Burning Bridges, from the war film Kelly's Heroes. Then it wasn't. And now, again, it is.

*

I think it is also the sound of the earth. Not the earth revolving round the sun, or round someone – a brother, a sister, a mother, a father. Nor is it the sound of the hurt. Rather, it's the actual sound of the earth, and digging. We were always digging dirt.

So close to last words: 'We were always digging dirt.'

We were always digging dirt, so the soundtrack is a shovel penetrating the topsoil earth and moving it.

Sort of a SCHH-K-K-K, then a sprinkle.

Digging dirt, building mounds of earth which sunk in the rain or were ploughed away by a farmer who'd lost himself in search of tubercular badgers, or a den of foxes to burn down, because it's easier to feel in control when your subordinates, though they may possess impressive biological weapons, don't have syringes to inject them with, or thumbs.

With that in mind, the sound could be a bicycle freewheel spinning. Click-click-clicking. Or a spanner round a headset, turning. Or a bottom bracket burning as you're racing down a hill. Or children playing soldiers. Shouting orders. Digging dirt. Gravel pits. Army boots. The soundtrack shooting up your arm with a shivering sting as a horsefly drinks your blood. A little death which comes as quickly as a lip to a wasp sting. That first jump in a river. That drink of liver fluke water. My father spent Seventies summers being avoided by his parents, on cadet training camps with his brother, where men groomed child soldiers and ruling classes to stand in line. My father was the last one standing–

He'd recalled, after I was born, when he'd lost all optimism, 'All I've achieved is a son, then you. But everyone I know without a vagina is a father (except your uncle, though he may as well have one too (ha!), so the best advice I'd give you, if you want to prove yourself, and I mean really PROVE yourself, is to pick up the gun and breathe out as you pull the trigger.'

It gets bigger.

–and hadn't stepped back quick enough when the sergeant requested a man (ha!) to carry the Bren.

My dream. Heavy, but with a high rate of fire.

Uncle Jim was upstream. And not yet an uncle. So Jim was

upstream with the regimental cadet force public schoolboy swimming team–

Clothing optional, predictably rejected.

–and had taken it upon himself, after having successfully bathed with his classmates while their World War Two era uniforms, boots, helmets, webbing and outdated blank-firing weapons stood huddled together in tipi formations, feeling drab, to explore the area upstream with a cup of milky World War Two era tea from a camping stove kettle, in his hand. All he found was the body of a dead deer, rotting partially into and out of the river.

He didn't have the heart to tell the other toy soldiers, as a lower class of male than his father. He did, however, make a mental note to tell his brother not to drink the water fresh; to boil everything on the stove from now on into the future. Meanwhile, behind the great trunk of an old yew tree, his brother, who just wanted to be left alone, was aiming a blank-firing Lee-Enfield No.4 at his foot, closing his eyes and hoping for a superficial wound.

*

What's that?' says Willow, spilled on my sofa like a feather-filled duvet in winter. 'Oh that?' I say whilst standing at the window where I've been smoking and thinking about blowing up the Shard, 'that's an M16A2 assault rifle.'

To field-strip your M16A2 assault rifle you must first pop out the two pins which connect the lower receiver to the upper receiver. The pins are located above the pistol grip and the magazine well. Once removed, slide the upper receiver (attached to the barrel) off the lower receiver (attached to the rear stock, grip and trigger). Slide the bolt assembly out by pulling back the charging handle. Remove the pin on the right side of the bolt carrier to free the firing pin, then remove the bolt from the bolt carrier by ejecting the bolt pin. You can only eject the bolt pin once the firing pin has been freed.

Clean, then reverse to reassemble.

Willow's wearing one of my t-shirts. The one that says, 'Heisenberg Says Relax' on it. She's also holding a glass of wine. It's weird. 'How long do you think it would take to get shot if I went into the Underground with that?' I say, pointing at the M16A2 assault rifle, which is squashed behind the fake leather Ikea armchair, teasing the wall with its black metal barrel, flaunting its flash suppressor.

'I think that depends a lot on which tube station you took it to,' says Willow, drinking.

'How about Bethnal Green?' I say. 'The tiles. The old rails. The draught.'

The soundtrack could be an echo.

'There're often a lot of people there,' I say. 'Quick response time from the police, but I may get to shoot at least one person in the leg before they kill me.'

Willow picks up the bottle. It's a top-shelf sauvignon blanc and I can still just about afford it. 'Do you think I've put on weight?' I ask her.

'A little,' she says. 'I thought you were walking more?'

'I haven't moved all day.'

I can hear a whimper. A night-time shiver of children's laughter.

'When I was younger I had a Heckler & Koch MP5SD3.'

'What's that?' she says.

'A type of German machine pistol.'

Willow rolls her eyes.

'You could call it a sub-machine gun, too. Do you know what SD stands for?'

She shakes her head.

'SD stands for Schalldämpfer. That means sound suppressor. It had four joules of power and was made out of ABS plastic, except for the stock which was part metal, as was the barrel. The stock was collapsible. Shatterable, too, if you dropped it. Which I did. Or rather, my mother knocked it off the arm of a chair, where I'd left it after playing with my brother.'

'She probably did that on purpose,' says Willow.

'Maybe. Guns make her nervous.'

'What would you wear, if you infiltrated a tube station?'

'I hadn't thought that far.'

'A suit would be good.' Willow stands up. 'Or a puffer jacket, padded out with bags of rice.' She walks towards me.

'Wild rice?'

She shrugs. 'How about quinoa?' she asks me, grinning. 'The cops would definitely go for that.' She rolls a cigarette impatiently.

Willow is pressed up against me. Willow's arm is reaching behind me. Willow's mind is on the no-longer-used balcony, popping off–

'How many bullets does it carry?'

Willow's fingers round the barrel.

Willow's pulling out the rifle.

I light another cigarette and say, 'Well, it's a bb gun, but a real one takes thirty.'

Willow's standing four feet away from me now, holding the M16, pointing it at me. 'It feels flimsy,' she says. 'How do you fire it?'

'To cock your M16A2 assault rifle you simply pull back the

charging handle.'

'Like this?' Willow pulls back the charging handle with her right hand. With her left hand she holds the forestock. Her shoulder is cradling the rear.

'That's right.'

'You'll need to research the depths of the stations,' she says.

Get down on your knees.

'What'll you do until the police arrive? Kill everybody?'

'It could be an elaborate joke,' I say. 'We–'

'We?'

'–could equip people with blood packs.'

'Explosive blood packs?' says Willow

'Yes,' I tell her, proudly, 'explosive blood packs.'

Look directly up at me.

'Too much,' she says. 'They'll shoot you for sure if they see anyone who looks dead. Won't be much of a joke then, will it.'

'I'd need wrapping paper, or something similar,' I tell her, 'in order to get the rifle down there. If I took one step out of my front door with that thing, the police would be there.'

Open your mouth.

'Then we may as well just shoot you now,' says Willow, staring down the barrel at me.

Says Willow, gripping the rifle with whitening knuckles.

Says Willow, pulling the shitty, fake plastic trigger.

Pop.

Willow smiles. 'It's just as well it's a toy, then,' she says, putting it back behind the sofa before sitting down on the floor in front of me. 'Why do you still have it?' she asks.

I say, 'I don't know.'

'Aren't you cold?' she asks.

I say, 'No.'

'You have an erection,' she says.

'I know. I used to have an S10 1986 issue gas mask, too.'

'Why'd you get rid of it?'

'Couldn't breathe when I wore it.'

'Sounds perfect,' says Willow.

BEDSPRINGS

The power cable to the bedside light twitches every time Willow's heart beats. We flipped the mattress before we tried to sleep. The bedside light is attached to the headboard. The power cable runs horizontally from the socket above the skirting board. It has a small switch about three quarters of the way along it. When we flipped the mattress a load of dust blew up in a grey four-cornered mushroom cloud. Willow said, 'When was the last time you cleaned under there?'

'I've been meaning to have a bonfire,' I told her.

She said, 'Cut the crap.'

We didn't bother to make the bed back up. We'd had a lot of wine. And my nose keeps dribbling. Could be blood. Internal rupture. Body knows better than me. Wants out. Forces me to keep checking to see if my snot is red. I said to Willow, 'I don't want to get snot all over the pillow case.' It was already on her shirt collar. Willow stripped everything bare. Then she lay on the bed, spread her arms, threw her feet, and said, 'It hasn't changed.'

I lie with my mouth open, warm inside the bare duvet. Polyester bobbles exfoliate. Sweat glands are open and on parade. Follicles dilate. Pave the way. I roll over. Scrotum enveloping my inner thigh like feather down or clear honey on a hot day. I reach towards the bedside table behind me for a tissue. There are none. A police car drives past with its lights flashing but no siren. The power cable to the bedside light twitches. I can hear Willow's heart beating through the bedsprings. Revitalised. Calm. Jurassic Park glass of water in relentless metal springs singing her sonar blip.

I envy her.

Start drooling more.

Heart like a rubber ball bouncing off the bedroom walls.

Always coming back.
Oh, I envy her.

'It doesn't matter,' I'd said. And like lead in a river sank down behind her on the bed. We didn't have sex. We just lay, me lining the edge of the bed while her breath kept ramming the wall.

I suck in so aggressively I half expected my frontal lobe to detach. Down throat. Hit lung peninsular with meteoric power. Bleed. Colour of migraine. Rot. Bridging the gap between having a stroke and knowing you're probably going to have one eventually. Be reduced to a vegetative state in a care home. The police car has stopped moving. Its lights block the street lamps and turn the room into blue blood, flashing.
Maybe they're finally coming for me.

I get up and go to the bathroom. Sit on the toilet, lid down, naked. Goose pimples. Try blowing my nose. No blood on the paper. Not even a common cold. Still, something's wrong. My hands are shaking. Think about running a quick bath but I can't stand up. Feet glued to the floor. Freezing. I rub my face, my hair. Try listening for something, anything. Dead sister. Weeping sister. She wept for me earlier. Gun in my mouth. Now nothing. Something's wrong. I'm completely alone.
The door opens. Willow stands there fully clothed, rubbing her eye. 'I think I'm going to go,' she says.

Harry Gallon

AND THE DOCTOR ASKS MY MOTHER IF SHE SELF-HARMS

On the day my brother got married I was in a lecture. It was a hot day. Rain suits London better. My brother was in a registry office somewhere and I was trying to pay attention to the professor who was introducing us to our dissertation proposals.

I was struggling to hear because the room I was sitting in was hot. It was a large room but it felt small. It felt like I was sitting inside a cowrie shell that'd washed up on a beach. And I was trying harder not to fall asleep. Back then, every time I fell asleep I had the same recurring dream in which I died. I wasn't even lying in bed. I was sitting in a foldable chair. But the glare from the glass bottle eyes of my little sister, twisting boredom and rigor mortis between her dead little fingers in that lecture theatre, cold as latent air conditioning, sweaty as corpses in the sun, kept my heart rate supernaturally high, though not frightened.

'It's relieving,' she whispered, 'death.'

I was biting my lip.

'Feels like paradise,' she said. 'But not like heaven.'

Rolling my eyes.

'More like you're just on holiday. Like you're sitting on the hot dry sand of a tropical beach–'

Digging soil skin with fingernails.

'–while the bother of living is a faraway thing.'

My ankles were itching profusely. I had an appointment with the university counsellor and would have to leave early, then dinner with Willow. It was hot and my blood has always been tasty. 'Let me get that for you,' said my sister, on the floor, knees bent legs folded arms out hands holding my ankles, dead ripped brown fingernails scratching the mosquito bites I'd woken up with. 'They're symmetrical,' she said to me teasingly, then took off my shoes and took off my socks in the row at the back of the lecture hall. I'd put my phone on airplane mode so I didn't know that my brother was getting married. Somewhere, in a registry office, with just Stephanie, whom I'd only met twice, and the junior mechanic my brother employed as a witness.

I wasn't exactly moving. I wasn't exactly trying to stop my sister from scratching the itch on my ankles. I turned my head a little, maybe, just to see if her actions were attracting attention, but all I got were looks from other students who'd noticed me looking at them.

'They're getting redder,' she'd said, then, holding my bare feet close to her and stroking the area around the bites I'd received during the night. 'That tickles,' I said as my sister slid closer and began groping my toes with the crisp batter of her decomposed tongue. She was running her dry, flaky hands all around my shin bones and poking her nose against the hum of blood which had begun retreating back up towards my heart, beating faster as I tried not to laugh. 'Could you hold this, please?' I said to her, waving a book in her face while I tried to pick up my bag. My knuckles had turned white and I was gripping one of the arm rests at the side of the foldable auditorium seat while the professor–

"You might get a 2:1, but you won't get a First."

–was clicking faster and faster through slides. My spine had gone straight ,and there was no way I could stop squirming without alerting the girl in the seat nine feet away from me of what, if anything, was happening.

Click.

My sister was stroking my knees. I leant to the side and

reached into my bag. Pulled out a bottle of water. It was warm and tasted of chlorine. 'Just hold this for me, now, please,' I said loudly, standing, shivering in prickly heat before actually giving my sister anything to hold. Book and notepaper spilling. Finding it hard to breathe. Water bottle lid fell and rolled down the stepped hill to the front of the hall without hitting anyone's feet.

Bent slightly in the middle, I dithered off to the back of the auditorium and went out through the back door.

I didn't notice the piss on the floor of the toilet, even though my feet were bare. I was breathing heavily and staring at myself in the huge wall-sized mirror, whispering: 'We're always together. We're always together.'

It'd been okay at first, for years a nuisance. Now she was a pain.

I turned airplane mode off. Triggered the motion sensor on the tap. Wash hands. Return to seat. My phone vibrated. There was a picture of my brother with a haircut and Stephanie in a chintz dress and a message that said, 'GUESS WHAT?'

Back in the auditorium everyone else had left. I sat down in my chair next to where my sister had left my shoes and socks, preferring herself to rock back and forth somewhere else rather than wipe the piss off my toes. The mosquito bites on my ankles were meningitis red, the plains of skin white because my blood had not been invited back down from my ventricles yet.

When I finally arrived at the counsellor's office, her door was locked.

*

'It's gorgeous,' said my mother, who'd transformed over the

previous year-and-a-half into a flute glass of cheap sparkling wine, an impatient sigh, an itchy foot healing after pulling a muscle whilst walking. She'd started walking. She needed the practice. She held her new daughter-in-law's hand and examined the ring her eldest son hadn't asked her advice on before buying. 'I just wish you could've told us first,' she'd said, then, whispering so that Stephanie couldn't hear, 'you could've had your grandmother's,' which was just about the only valuable thing she owned. It was the Easter holidays and I'd come home for a few days. My brother was there with his new wife. So was Gentleman Jim, though he was obviously alone and looking frail. Lunch outside. Even my grandmother. Excavated from her hole and unwittingly breaking Kettle Chips into a pot of taramasalata.

'You really should have told us,' said our father angrily, fingers prickling with heat and a chin that shook the parasol.

'We wanted to do it our own way,' said my brother, without meeting his eye. Black fingernails. Jim sat silently in the corner, looking older and wheezing. 'He's had too much already,' said our father, raising his eyes at his own brother in an attempt to show mine that he couldn't hear, rather than wouldn't, the reasons why they'd chosen not to invite any family members. 'Probably a good thing that Jim didn't go along,' said Dad, 'what with him always threatening to bring one of his shady friends.' He laughed. Looked at me. 'And how's that girl of yours?'

'She's fine.'

'Makes the rent cheaper, eh.'

I didn't reply. My mother limped to the fridge and said, 'Who wants another glass?'

*

Dad drove my grandmother back to the home a few hours later,

Jim back to his. Brother and Stephanie were in our old room upstairs which my parents had converted, since we'd left, into a spare. Removed concave and cabin beds. Replaced curtains and hurtled a second-hand queen-size up the stairs. I'd be on the sofa. Stood on the patio with a cigarette, waiting for everyone to go to bed.

My mother sat on one of the kitchen chairs by the back door. It was almost dark. The sky was changing and she was convalescing between exercises in preparation. Waiting for the day when I'd graduated, would no longer require her signature on my tenancy agreements in guarantee of rent payment. Waiting to leave.

'Did you say something?' she asked, as I watched my dead sister, floppy and dripping, and eyeing me through a hole in one of our mother's large terracotta flowerpots, which I'd accidentally made with a black widow slingshot when I was younger.

'I was just thinking,' I said, lying down on the grass by the old overgrown garden hedge, 'about a dream I had recently.' I neglected to mention her intention to leave because I didn't want to discourage her.

'What dream was that?' she asked, rubbing her arms with a G&T.

'I dreamt that I'd been hanged,' I said. My mother didn't say anything. She kept rubbing but no longer her skin, more at the sky and contrails. Stubborn. Unlikely that she'd ever rely on a man to make her day again. She'd do it. She'd leave. I knew it. The dead foetus of her daughter could prove it, but I didn't want to ask. In her silence I looked at my mother, feeling very twenty-one. Just on the cusp, but not quite ready. 'I'm sorry,' I said, 'I didn't mean to–'

'Why'd they hang you?' she asked, flexing her toes.

'I don't know,' I said.

Could've been infanticide. Could've been manslaughter that

hadn't happened yet.

'And did you die?' she asked me. My mother was itchy. I could see her fingering her wedding ring with less care than my father gave the washers he kept in his tool box.

So like a man.

'It's a bad omen,' she said, 'to die in a dream.'

'Well,' I said, feeling balmy, 'I did. But it was a good thing. I remember being led to a large wooden platform through a crowd of all my friends. But they were made-up friends. Dream friends. Some people I recognised from real life, but otherwise they were made-up. And the light was strange. Like now. Both dawn and dusk simultaneously. Everything was blue and–'

The flowerpot exploded. Fertilised soil and terracotta went everywhere except on my mother, who lay, feet up, waiting, having not even noticed. The church bells down in the village were tolling loudly, then stopped as if suddenly muted.

'There's a cold spot at the bottom of the hill,' said my mother. 'Your father walks through it on his way home from the village. I think he passes through the spirits of the dead.' She shook her head slowly and sniffed. 'He thinks I'm stupid.' She upturned her G&T. The remaining ice and pinched lime wedge dropped carelessly onto what was left of her once decorative flowerbed. It had become a graveyard for plastic soldiers I'd long since left to grow brittle in the sun. 'How's your foot?' I asked, looking at her toes. Both legs were stretched out. One, the left, was wrapped in a Tubigrip that partially covered some dark stains on her skin left by her cheap leather shoes. 'It's fine. Not really much you can do, apart from rest,' she said. 'The doctor was more interested in my arms.'

We both looked at my mother's arms.

'He asked me if I self-harm.'

We both laughed.

'I just told him I'm bad at cooking.'

There was a pause.

Then my mother said, 'Your father will be home soon.' She stood up. 'I'm sure you'll be ready to get out of here, too.' She stood, limped over, trying not to put too much pressure on her foot, and kissed me on the head. 'You need a shower,' she said. 'There's soil in your hair.'

It was dark when my brother came outside. He was holding a toothbrush. He said, 'I'm sorry.'

I said, 'For what?'

He said, 'I should've invited you.'

'It doesn't matter,' I said. I took a drag, dropped my fag into the terracotta pot. Empty. Sister evacuated. 'I'm happy for you,' I said. There was a pause. 'Though, I didn't think you'd do anything like this.'

'Get married?'

'Yes.' I reached into my pocket for some tobacco. 'You want one?'

My brother said, 'No.' He coughed. 'How's university?'

'It's fine, but I don't want to be there anymore.'

'What about your girlfriend?'

'Willow? I don't know. I think she's losing interest.'

'So drop out.'

'I don't want to come back here.'

'Mum wouldn't mind. She just wants you to be happy.'

'That's the problem. Besides, I'm almost finished.' Another pause. My brother shoved his toothbrush into his mouth and Stephanie came out with some water. 'Did you tell him?' she said. My brother held up a finger.

'Tell me what?' I asked.

My brother spat into the flowerbed, showering the plastic soldiers. Stephanie handed him the glass of water. He sipped. She said, 'I'm pregnant.'

My brother spat again.
The soil was an Oreo milkshake.
'You're the first person we've told,' he said.
'Congratulations.'
Stephanie smiled, kissed my brother on the cheek then left.
'Jim's leaving,' my brother said. 'I overheard him talking to Mum in the kitchen.'
'Did he ask her to go with him?'
'What?'
'Is it to do with their affair?'
My brother stepped a little closer, shook his head. He said, 'What are you talking about?'
'Why is Jim leaving?' I asked.
'Because he's ill,' my brother said. 'You know that.'

three

Harry Gallon

ROCK POOLS

'I bet his career caught up with him,' said my sister. She was squatting in a pair of clear pink sparkly jelly shoes, poking a dead fish in the eye. 'But the Canary Islands? It's all volcanic rock. High spots. Nowhere to hide.'

I was standing at the sea shore, my toes curled round the edge of a rocky shelf which dove six feet down towards a rocky sea bed. The tide was out, and the Atlantic Ocean only just made it over the rock wall to cover my ankles.

'Where do you think the bullet will enter his body?' said my sister.

'What bullet?'

'You're right. It'll have to be a knife.'

'Oh God –'

'But then–'

'–not this–'

'–that makes–'

'–again.'

'–no sense.'

I took a deep breath. 'It's going to happen slowly,' I said. Or maybe I didn't say anything. I was staring at the boulders on the sea bed. They'd been shaped by the water. Smoothed. Piled one on top of the other as they fell into the ocean. Risen. Boulders which had been piled on and on and green and blue and which would, too, keep rising. Six feet between these boulders and me above the surface, which was a clean face in a morning window. Just little caves and cracks between each rock that made up the floor. A labyrinth in which tiny creatures could get lost and keep swimming without ever reaching the bottom.

'It's not that often your uncle is an assassin,' my sister told me, as though the thought had never occurred. As though I hadn't lain awake at night wondering if Gentleman Jim might one day kill my father then marry my mother. 'I know what you're going to say: "He's not my uncle." Well, I'm here too, aren't I? You shoved me in your hand luggage and brought me on that plane,' said my sister, as she held the fish's eye on the end of a salt-dried stick before flicking it into the sea.

I hadn't been home much since we celebrated my brother's marriage. By this point his first child had been born.

It's a boy.

'What do you think happened to this fish?' said my sister from beneath a white cotton sun hat. She was tapping its xylophone ribs. Running a pudgy finger up and down vertebrae chimes. Or maybe they were the metal railings outside a primary school. 'Do you think something had been chasing it? Or maybe someone was trying to catch it? And the fish bit the hook but fought the fisherman and broke the line. Except the struggle used up all its will to keep on living, so it swam into a rock pool and waited for the tide to go out and the sun to dry the water, then died.'

I hadn't been home because there wasn't one. My mother had finally left. My father wouldn't get dressed unless he had a bathroom to fit. It took Jim nearing death to get him to put his shoes on.

'Do you like my dress?' said my sister, whose fingers I could smell from where I stood and can still smell from here. 'It's what our mother would've dressed me in at roughly the age of four, had I, you know, lived.' I was still standing on the edge of the shelf. A dozen tiny fish swam in the ankle-deep water that made it over the top of the rock. The rock was black and rough as pumice. I put my weight on one foot then twisted it ninety degrees, exfoliating as the skin was shed like sand blown from a windy beach.

'Why do you think he chose for it to be here?' said my sister.

'What?'

'His safe house. For when a job went wrong or his own boss turned on him. They'd have sent another assassin to kill him, but Gentleman Jim can't be killed by just any human being.'

'Maybe he chose this place to have a gun fight,' I said.

'You could be right,' said my sister. 'Remember the road on the drive in from the airport? Rocky outcrops to knock heads on. There'd be hired guns, fresh from the supermarket towns around London, who'd been flown out by known employers of cockney assassins after being pushed out of their old territories by a higher price of living. Bodies subject to inflation. They'd know him, Gentleman Jim. They'd have pulled the knife together. Cut throats and worn gloves and filled Tupperware bowls with his blood.'

'Jim's not a serial killer,' I told her, feeling older and annoyed. Feeling exactly how my brother felt, I suppose, whenever I spoke about Jim. 'He'd never take pleasure in murder.'

'Wouldn't he?' she said.

There was a long pause. I used that long pause to ignore her. The long pause was a vast hazy cruise liner passing from left across my picture to right into the frame which, actually, was a hibernating marina at the other end of the beach. Any second now the ship would be directly in line with my sister's flicked fish eye, floating dull as Fahrenheit sky and the blurry boat that passed. All sea-smoothed glass. Not as sharp as the broken Budweiser I'd circumnavigated in bare feet round the corner of the rocks at this end of the beach, near a tiny football stadium and its perimeter of palm trees. An old stone home still further on and nearer the mountain that would shadow it if the sun didn't stay directly at noon all day. Keeping the Spanish indoors so the English get pink on the beaches, though it was January and I'd seen barely any of them as it was.

'Don't you remember the way he grinned when he held that man in front of him,' said my sister, 'while we watched from the hollowed-out yew tree? And that young man he tied to the bed with rope?'

How he'd loosened his tie.

How he'd held his glass of orange light and looked out of the window and sighed, as though he'd seen me, knew he couldn't stop me being curious but no, nephew, this was not the way to go about it.

'He's a tortured soul,' said my sister, feigning romance. 'A tragic figure no one could love or abhor, not even a mother.'

Jim had let go. Jim had let go and let go and let go. It was my father's idea to visit him. They often spoke on the phone. Get out of that house. Abroad for a year. Can you honestly tell me you didn't see it coming? She's happier, and so will you be, in time. Jim coughed a lot. His skin looked baggy. He didn't have much time.

'He knows they'll find him here,' said my sister.

She was kissing the dead fish's head.

She sounded older.

Her voice was deeper.

Grown twenty years. Grown taller. Grown breasts and thighs and thick skin on the balls of her feet.

'Jim WANTS them to kill him,' she said.

She was deeper.

The cruise liner had by now almost completely crossed the vista, from the cliff at the side of the mountain towards the marina.

My sister said, 'Jim isn't dying. Jim's running. Jim lied.'

I stood, feet side by side sliding along the landscape, feeling alien. The boulders were open and the ocean darker off the side of the shelf, while the tide, that could, reached up and flirted with the rock, and kept my feet in cool, salty socks. I wasn't wearing anything else except trunks and sun cream.

I smelled like a baby.

Earlier in the day I'd been swimming and found what I thought were the remains of an ancient civilisation. It was about twelve feet below the surface, partially buried. But ten seconds before drowning I realised it was just a piece of old pipeline.

I decided to leave my sister with her rotting fish and walk a little further along the rock shelf, to where the rock itself grew darker and higher the closer it got to the foot of the cliff. I stopped where the rock shelf was at least three feet above the surface and the sea could no longer tease me. The rock shelf here wasn't slippery. It was parched and sharp as the beak of the bird which had heard my sister's fish pop its last bubble in those shallows, then glided down lazily to peck at it.

I looked to the right, towards the town and the beach and the marina, where the masts were obscuring the horizon and the wake of the cruise liner was tickling the boats at mooring. I looked to the left and saw a bare-chested young woman sunbathing on a tiny stone beach, right beneath the tall cliff at the foot of the mountain. The young woman saw me looking and turned onto her front.

'You don't think he can just retire, do you?' said my sister. 'It's not that simple. It can't be that simple. Not for a person like him.'

'Like who?' I said, though I knew.

'Like Jim,' said my sister. 'The world won't let him have a happy ending. The world, the old world, the one that he grew up in, the one that made him, has already rejected him.'

She paused.

I said nothing.

'Do you really still think that they are going to kill him?' I asked, though I didn't even know who *they* were anymore.

'Yes,' said my sister. 'With a high-velocity rifle, probably. In the arms of a good marksman, positioned at the top of that mountain,' pointing, 'while Jim's sitting at a café down by the beach one morning.'

'Seems more likely,' I said, 'that he'll slowly waste away. Just like Grandma.'

'No, that's what'll happen to your father,' said my sister. 'Jim's more like your brother. Or rather, your brother's more like Jim.'

'What do you mean?'

'You'll see.'

'So who does that make me like?' I asked, repositioning myself to face her only to find that she'd gone. My heels were kissing the edge of the higher rock shelf. I couldn't tell how deep the water was there. I looked over my shoulder and could see the green boulders. Their alleyways and cellars and all that could've led on endlessly to nowhere. I faced forward, with my chin up and my back straight and my arms up at right angles, towards the mountain, the house, and the palm trees round the stadium, then let myself fall.

The ocean had been sunbathing all day. It was warm and lacklustre by now. I could see through it like fibre optic cable. Zeroed in on the waving shape of a half-naked woman standing on the shelf above me, looking down. She stood there for what seemed like hours as I sank to the boulders. When she jumped in it seemed too sudden. She grabbed me and dragged me and swam me to the edge of the shelf, where she spoke at me in Spanish.

She looked a lot older, up close.

When I climbed out I couldn't see my sister. She'd left the fish bones to decompose further in the sun, having picked the flesh off the head and dropped it, in chunks, one by one, in a trail that led back to town.

I went and found Jim who was sitting at a table outside a cafe by the sea wall. He was drinking a coffee. Looking pale. I sat down opposite him on the chair where I'd left my towel before I'd walked down the beach. There was a packet of cigarettes on the table and as I lit one Jim said, 'Those'll kill you, you know,' before coughing for nine seconds straight.

'Why did you decide to come here?' I asked him.

He took a sip of coffee.

'You know, the first week I was here,' he said, 'I was in a bar just up the road there,' pointing. 'I'd been walking around, trying to get an idea of where things are, what time the shops open, you know. It was late and I found a bar. It has beaded curtains for doors when it's open, and a pool table. I hadn't played pool in years. Not since I was your age, living in London.'

'I didn't know you lived in London.'

'That's right. I worked for a wood veneer manufacturer, as a driver.'

He coughed.

His skin looked transparent.

He was thinner.

'So I went in because I wanted to play some pool, and the owner of the bar challenged me to a game.'

'Who won?'

'I did,' said Jim. 'And as a reward the owner offered me a large shot of his homemade liquor. I can't remember how strong it was or what it was called. So we drank it (it was quite sweet) and he asked me, in quite lazy English, the same question you just asked me.'

'And?'

'Wait. He said, "Nobody comes here. No tourists. No English. This place doesn't even have a hotel."'

'What did you say?' I asked.

'I just said, "Exactly."'

My father was standing near the entrance to the marina, fishing by the harbour wall as the tide began to come in. 'What about my mother,' I asked Jim, who'd shrunk.

'I should think she's happier, now,' he said. 'Does that surprise you?'

I looked at my father all the way over there and said, 'No.'

'She was always very good to me, your mother. And I love her very much, as does he.' And Jim looked towards him too. 'But they'd been together since they were very young.'

'Like my brother and Stephanie?'

'Yes, I suppose. But your brother is older, in certain ways. He knows better already, really, because he grew up in a different age.'

Pause.

'Did you ever have an affair with her?'

'Your mother?' Jim laughed, started spooning half-melted sugar from his coffee glass and asked about my new job.

'Good pay for a graduate,' I told him.

My father walked over empty handed. 'Had a big one, there,' he said. 'Little bastard broke my line.'

Jim nodded, began coughing again. Said, 'I think I'll go for a swim.'

'Stay near the shore,' my father said. 'And watch your breathing. Otherwise I'm coming in to get you.'

THE SECRET LIVES OF HIRED GUNS – PART TWO

Jim died a year later. Not long before my brother. My mother told me. She phoned me. 'Are you sitting down?' she'd said. 'I've got some bad news.' I could tell she wasn't sure how to carry herself. I could almost see it. She was sitting in her new car, talking to me via Bluetooth. The signal kept being interrupted. She spoke slowly, as though there was no time for anything else.

It hit her hard.

'Hold on,' said my sister, who was with me at the time. 'Let me guess: Jim's head has been exploded.' I held my mother on the line, phone against shoulder.

'What?' I asked her. 'How do you know?'

'I've always known,' she said. 'I've just been waiting for it to happen.'

I was on a lunch break. New job. Had just been to Pret and was sitting on a curb near Liverpool Street, chewing a sandwich and waiting for my coffee to cool down. It was good timing. I looked at my sister suspiciously. Swallowed. Put the phone back to my ear. My mother said, 'Hold on, sorry.' She was parking her car. 'Right. Okay. Jim's dead.'

My sister leapt. Tore her tights. Frightened a gang of pigeons. 'I knew it,' she said. 'They got him.' She was much bigger than usual, had camouflaged herself pencil skirt charcoal and concrete. Cracked cackling mouth corners and eye posters on billboard nostrils flaring when she widened everything and said, 'He must've died instantly. A rifle shot of that calibre would've taken more than just his crown off. It would have wrenched his soul free.'

It began to rain.

'It's no surprise, of course,' said my mother, after she'd been silent for a while and I'd been silent for a while too. She was sniffing. 'And it's for the best.'

'Are you okay?' I asked.

'I'm fine. Just stopped for a breather.'

'Where are you going?'

'Home,' she said. She'd been living in a flat near Colchester. Had wanted to be closer to my brother, Stephanie, and the children after she finally left my father. She'd got a job with a travel agency, selling package holidays. Buying Indian takeaways and walking her rescue dog. 'Took the afternoon off,' she said.

'I'm going to come and see you. I'll speak to my boss. Take the day off tomorrow.'

'Oh, no,' she said, 'I'm fine. It's not like we didn't know this was coming.'

'Why didn't Dad tell me?'

She coughed.

'He's gone back out there,' she said, 'to, um, collect the remains.'

'That's bullshit,' said my sister, who'd bitten the feet off a pigeon and was watching it flap around, dragging bloody streamers across the pavement. 'She's lying.' I'd taken my tie off, or at least loosened it slightly. I said to my sister, impatiently, 'What do you mean?'

'Your father didn't go out there to get Jim's body,' she said. 'Your father went there to kill him.'

YOUR BATH ISN'T DEEP ENOUGH

I got fired from my job today. I don't like loose ends. I like closure. You can drown in a few centimetres of bath water, and people would forever say, 'Of all the liquids his parents spilled to enable their child to die, this was the way he decided?' Like you're still waiting in the tub. Turning into a fish while the water evaporates. Suffocating. Rot.

I love you.

At least you tried.

I got fired. My phone rang, with something garbled about new directions. Life changes following large, unexpected upheavals. It went like this: 'Listen.'

'Yes?'

'I'm from HR.

'You've been off for three months.

'We're all very sorry about what happened.

'But you haven't responded to our emails or answered our calls.

'We need to discuss your future with the company.

'We feel that it's time to draw a line and inform you that we no longer consider your contribution necessary.

'We're letting you go.

'You will, of course, be given redundancy pay. And we'd be glad to provide you with a reference.

'Do you have any questions?'

Click.

I've been systematically unsubscribing from estate agency and concert ticket mailing lists. I've been lying for hours in the bath. I've been lying FOR HOURS dreaming up reckless unconventional shopping lists that I'm never going to fulfil. Topping up the temperature with hosepipes of hot water and toes to try and warm my digestive system in the hope that the heat will help all the shit that's become impacted in my lower intestine slide out. Coffee and cigarettes. Coffee and cigarettes. Turns out it's just gas. Googling reasons why my stomach gets bloated. Allergens, maybe. Should eat three meals a day. And why is it taking so long for the cut I got from the bicycle chainring to heal? I think I'm bleeding internally. Ruptured stomach. Fissured anus. Blood seeping out like fishy air from a pinch flat. Patch it up. Everything's fine.

I've become what people rely on when they get home from work. Something dull. Something to fulfil their need to be looked at. To be smiled at. To be cried at and told, 'Thank you.' And told, 'Thank you.' And then to tell everyone, 'You've helped me. Now everything's going to be fine.'

You're a normal human being, for once. A normal human being. Needed by someone so in need that all he can think about is a few centimetres of water. And what his mother would say if someone called her and told her that's the way her last remaining child decided to die.

Fine.

At least it wasn't a gun.

At least she wouldn't be the one to find me.

I've become what people rely on, only there's no one relying on me.

My phone rings again. I left it resting on the radiator. Back-facing camera covered with electrical tape. Vibrations worming their way to the cracked lino floor. I reach, dry my hand with the towel by the door. Seems laughable to care. Hit speaker. 'Hello Mum.'

'Darling,' she says. 'How're you?'

'I'm fine.'

'I spoke to Willow the other day.'

'You did?'

'She says she's concerned about you.'

'She is?'

'Very concerned.'

'We haven't spoken in a while.'

'I didn't know you two were seeing each other again.'

'We're not.'

'That's not what I meant.'

There's a pause. Slow gurgle air pocket from the pipe below the bath. Cracked plug. Dribbling water. Hit the hot tap to refill. So hot my feet feel cold. My mother says, 'Where are you?'

I say, 'I'm in the bath.'

'That's nice.'

'Are you alright?' I ask.

'Oh, you know me,' she says. 'It's never easy.'

'How're your feet?'

'They're not done carrying me yet.'

'I quit my job today.'

'You what?'

'It's fine. I don't want to be there anyway.'

'You're going to look for another one, though, aren't you?'

'Yes.'

'You promise?'

Another pause.

'Yes.'

I assume she's nodding. I know she's driving. She's always driving. Her reception's never good. She says, 'I'll do a nice, big online shop for you.'

She says, 'I'll send you some treats.'

She says, 'I think you should come and stay with me for a while.'

She says, 'I miss you.'

Harry Gallon

THE FIVE SECOND GAME – PART TWO

I was asleep when they found me at the side of the road. I was sleeping in the warm petroleum body fat glow of my combusting brother. Newly deceased. Newly killed by me. Head flipped over like the pickup truck he was still strapped into, eyes closed as though it was he who had decided now was a good time to play the Five Second Game.

Part Two.

It wasn't the fumes of the burning fuel tank contents or the dribbling, temperate human fat or the queer flow of tyre rubber which dropped like tired napalm onto the road, sizzling, and eventually caught the tarmac alight, threatening the wetness of the bramble bushes that held the disgruntled entrails of my mother's old green bike.

It'd been thrown from the truck on impact. Bounced like a dead baby's head, then relaxed, like me, in the foliage.

It wasn't the soft French kiss of the English rain on my forehead which put me to sleep, though it may have been the head wound. Or the shock of my leg breaking. Of my tibia snapping like a rifle report and my fibula bayoneting through my skin.

Crack.

Staying awake seemed like a chore, lying, as I was, where the road met the shore of the verge.

It could've been the prospect of still having to get to the crematorium, where my mother and father and other people's mothers and fathers and brothers and sisters and maybe some lingering grandparents in diapers had already gathered, to not only mourn one burning corpse, but to inform them all of another.

And besides, I already had a pyre.

It could just as easily have been The Mike Curb Congregation on the stereo, still playing Burning Bridges upside down in the upturned Toyota cabin. That had me smiling. Had me coughing to sing along until the acid in the battery underneath the inverted car bonnet started boiling, boiled over and exploded the electrics with a KA-FFT-FTT, sizzling. 'Must be the shock of the leg breaking,' said a voice above me. A stranger's voice. 'And the concussion.'

'Not to mention the death of his passenger,' said another stranger beside me. 'Boiled alive by their own combustion. What an awful, terrible way to–'

'Shh,' said the first voice. 'He's been unconscious since the accident. He doesn't know that the passenger's dead.' My eyelids kept flickering. I was trying to keep them closed but my eyelids kept on whispering to each other: 'Did you see what I just saw?'

'I'm not sure if he tried to save him.'

My eyelids were attempting to make the words I'd eventually say when I decided to pretend to wake up and make up some lie about how our Toyota pickup truck had ended up down the side of an embankment just off the M3.

'I thought it set fire to the tarmac?' said my left eyelid.

'And I thought it was on the M5?' said my right.

Everything went silent as the strangers above and beside me restarted: 'It's not a bad head wound,' one said. 'But that leg looks rather angry.'

'And he's lost both his eyebrows, poor bastard.'

KA-FFT-FTT-FFT-T-T

*

When you were dying I was dreaming of pillboxes. Say it out loud. When you were burning I was dreaming of pillboxes. Say it again. When you were melting I was taking apart a Bren gun. Field-stripping. And everything smelled of old paper, leather and gun oil.

Youngs 303.

Say it again.

When you–

Say it louder.

–were burning. When you were turning into carbon I was dreaming.

'You were sleeping,' said my sister. She, too, was also dead, but had been so for a while longer.

This you know.

'You weren't even trying to save him,' she said to me as we stood rickety in vertigo and on crutches staring out of a thirteenth floor hospital window. 'While you were dreaming,' she said, snakelike, grasping my leg, her head supporting an unimaginative ponytail, 'our brother was burning alive.'

'He was unconscious,' I said. 'He was already dead,' in a whisper, cracking, in case a real human would hear and take me back to the bed I was meant to be in. 'And he was never, ever your brother.'

My sister sighed. She said, 'I'm not surprised, what with your history. And our family's unlawful profession. Do you know what our mother did, when you elbowed me out of her womb? She mopped me up. She erased the blood.'

'That's not true,' I said. 'Her body reabsorbed you without her even knowing. I didn't push you out. You were never dead because your lungs were too underdeveloped to have even been able to take a breath. I wasn't a murderer.'

'Well,' she said, 'that's debatable. In any case, you are now.'

Tears started filling me eyes.

'Come now,' said my sister, sniffing my groin through the hospital gown, 'there's no need to get overly emotional. I didn't make you close your eyes, did I? It was always going to happen.'

She paused.

'You really need a wash.'

Outside, thirteen floors below us, a heavy excavator was separating chunks of stone and concrete from steel bars in a construction site that had once been the original hospital building. Everything was very quiet. The building I was in was very new. It had a helipad on the roof which I'd been air-ambulanced through a week before. The walls were white and the floor was drawn with coloured lines and nothing smelled yet. 'I bet it hurts,' said my sister, tapping the cast round my leg. 'Should you be standing on that yet?' She seemed much more alive after my brother had – what was it, passed to the other side? That's what they'd told me when I woke up earlier than they'd expected and asked the nurse attending to me, 'Where is he?'

'Where's who?'

'My brother.'

'Oh. Well, he's in the morgue, unfortunately,' he said, then walked off with a bag full of my piss.

'I suppose it should hurt,' said my sister, 'knowing what you've accomplished. And all in your early twenties. Very impressive.'

When we were teenagers my brother stole Uncle Jim's motorbike and crashed it through a hedgerow. It wasn't a hard fall, but the weight of the bike and his attempts to keep it upright fractured his left wrist. It wasn't a bad break. I went with him to the hospital. Our mother drove. The A&E department looked like a primary school. Underfunded and staffed by old women in dark dresses. Strong smell of disinfectant and vomit. Damp bricks and decrepit mortar. But now I was in concrete. Inches and inches thick. When my brother's body was burning I was unconscious and dreaming of pillboxes.

'You better be quick,' said my sister. 'Someone'll come to check on you, and you're not meant to be out of bed.'

She paused.

'Does it hurt?'

'Knowing what I did?'

'No,' she said. 'The metal pins they drilled into your leg.'

They did.

'They're going to keep holding you together. And not even time or the weather will break you.' She could barely conceal her laughter.

'Are you staying or going?' I asked her impatiently, still looking out of the window.

She said, 'You should've taken the train.'

I said, 'Yes, I should have.'

'There are pillboxes dotted all along the sides of British railways. A decaying reminder of better times when we all thought we were going to die together. The journey would've only taken you a couple of hours.'

'But we–'

'Got lazy?' she said, as I stood, aching, looking down at the man in the cab of the heavy excavator, picking up concrete and pieces of metal, tearing them apart from each other. 'YOU got lazy, though, didn't you.'

'–wanted to take the old Toyota. It used to belong to Jim, remember?'

'Whatever. You got tired. You'd had too much to drink, too much to sniff the night before. You closed your eyes.'

'He was driving from Essex and offered to pick me up.'

'You counted one, two, three, four – did he ask you to drive, or did you insist?'

There were a few doctors and nurses and paramedics and board members with brief cases smoking cigarettes in a circle outside the ambulance entrance to the hospital, thirteen floors below us. 'Do you think you could hit them from here?' said my dead little sister.

I said, 'Yes.'

'What rifle would you use?' she asked.

For a moment I was silent, but then I said, 'Mauser, 98K, Kar.'

'How many rounds does that hold?' she said.

And I told her, 'Five.'

THE DAY I KILLED MY BROTHER

It starts with a bicycle flying through the air. In slow motion. The Mike Curb Congregation on the stereo, Burning Bridges playing. Cutting back and forth between us in the car, turning over and over until the bicycle hits the ground.

I killed my brother on the same day as Gentleman Jim's funeral. I'd had to take the day off work, which suited me anyway because I'd drunk a lot the night before and was feeling pretty hungover. My brother was his own boss. He'd left his apprentice in charge of the motorbike garage he'd started a few years before and darted round his cottage, looking for a clean white shirt. He only had one. I have three. And everything he touched came up dirty. It was the grease and the engine oil buried beneath his fingernails. He also smelled like metal.

The funeral was held at a crematorium not far from the village we grew up in. Jim had wanted to be burned, apparently. He'd wanted his ashes to be scattered, nonchalantly as fag ends, in gutters along the roadway. Jim wasn't one for ceremony. And there wouldn't have been many people there, anyway. Two less, even, after my brother and I had spun out on the motorway and rolled away down an embankment.

It was the first day off I'd taken since starting my job after graduation. I could've taken the train from Paddington Station, but my older brother was driving from Essex and had offered to stop in London to give me a ride. He wasn't due to arrive at our meeting point until around 10 o'clock. I woke up at half-six. Picked a shirt. Black tie. The one that looks green in the light. My father had bought me some silver cufflinks for a graduation present. They must've cost him a lot. They have my initials embossed on them. When I got my first month's pay I went straight to Oxford Street and bought a suit and some smart shoes.

On the day I killed my brother I spent an hour looking at ties. I only have five.

I decided to change in the car. My brother said he'd drive into London as far as the North Circular, so we agreed to meet in Edmonton. I could've taken a train or a bus but I decided to ride our mother's old green Traffic Master. She hadn't wanted to take it with her when she left my father.

I stuffed my suit into a backpack with my smart shoes, tie, and shirt. Cufflinks my father gave me. Neither my brother nor I were planning on staying the night anywhere, least of all at our old home, so there was no need to pack a toothbrush.

'Aren't you sweaty?' my brother asked me.

I said, 'No. And it's raining, anyway.'

'Well,' he said, getting out. We were in a car park. 'I didn't bring any ratchet straps.'

I said, 'I'm sure it'll be alright.' I put the bike into the back of the old Toyota pickup truck. It bounced around on the hard suspension and lounged on the arches at stop lights. 'You could've shaved,' said my brother, as I batted his finger from the patches of hair under my chin. 'We'll stop at some services on the motorway so you can change.'

There was a pause.

There were roadworks near Brent Cross which had us stop-starting along rows of moped terraces and houses protected by dilapidated fences, and industrial estate wind turbine engines unwinding, as we, brothers, merged and merged again and when we got to the A40 we finally opened up to fifty, and stayed there until it became the M40 and we stopped for coffee. When I came out of the service station wearing my suit my brother was leaning against the car, guarding the bike, throwing me the keys after I said, 'Let me drive.'

'Remember when you stole Jim's motorbike?' I said. My brother was rubbing his thumb. 'They gave you a pink cast, right?'

He said, 'It was blue.' He said, 'Yeah, I do.'

Another pause.

'Do you ever feel like you weren't really there, when we were kids?'

'I didn't think I was anywhere else,' said my brother, flexing his index finger.

'You weren't there when Dad smacked us with his flipflop?'

The one with the rainbow strap.

'Or when he grabbed us by the back of our necks to wash our mouths out with soap?'

'Why are you asking me this?' said my brother, adjusting the rear view mirror.

'I can't see if you do that.'

'Sorry.'

'I feel like we've been waiting for this day for our entire lives,' I said. 'And now that it's here, I don't really believe it.'

'Have you heard from Dad?' said my brother.

Have you spoken to him? Has he telephoned you and told you what state the body is in? Was in, when they (who?) found him?

Was the head split open, losing brain?

Was the throat slit and bleeding?

Was it a mercy killing?

'Do you remember the name of the song that was in Kelly's Heroes?' I asked my brother, who was checking his phone.

He said, 'Yes.'

'Do you know how it happened?' I asked him, while he hummed in the rain and I drove. 'Because I'm thinking it was a single high-velocity round to the head.'

'Of course THIS had to be the weather today,' said my brother. 'The man retires to a hot Spanish island, and when he dies from natural,' looking at me, 'causes the family he was trying to escape from decide to bury him in the rain. In the English fucking rain.' He rolled his eyes.

'I don't think he was escaping us, was he?'

'Not you or me,' said my brother.

'And not our mother, either,' I said. 'He loved her, whether they had that affair or not.'

'How could that possibly have happened?' he said.

Something moved on the back seat.

'Do you ever wish you could mount a cannon on the front of your car?' I said. 'So you could blow all the traffic away?'

My brother laughed. 'How soon after it happened did Dad fly out there?' he said.

'He was there already,' I said.

'Who told you that?'

'It was–'

I turned around but the back seat was empty.

'Was it Mum?' asked my brother. 'I didn't realise they were talking.'

'She's with him now, isn't she, helping to sort everything out?'

My brother laughed. 'I can't get used to their being near each other, never mind get along' he said. 'Seems like they were never meant to have been together at all.'

'I suppose change follows naturally after large, unexpected upheavals.'

'There was nothing unexpected about Jim's death,' he said. 'Or the divorce. I suppose we can ask Dad when we get there, anyway.'

'Will you roll me a cigarette?'

'No.' He shook his head. 'I still can't believe those two.'

'Mum and Dad?'

'Dad and Jim. The love they had for each other. The closeness they shared as brothers, after what their own father put them through. How he treated Jim, and how Jim was treated by everyone who thought they knew him.'

'And?'

'And yet Dad still ended up resenting him.'

'Was that Jim's reason for leaving?'

He looked at me with impatience. 'Jim just wanted to die peacefully and in his own way. You know that already, so take whatever crap you've got stuck in your head and flush it.'

I sniffed.

'He just didn't want to waste away in front of us,' said my brother, 'like Granny.'

'How polite.'

*

The last thing my brother said to me was, 'Open your fucking eyes.' The last thing I said to my brother was, 'Want to have a go?' Everything that happened after that was noise. Not loud, white noise. Underwater noise. Ear infection noise. And muscle tension. The cracking of glass and then a great big loud HA HA HA darkness.

'We're coming off in a couple of miles,' said my brother.

'Do you remember the Five Second Game?' I asked him.

And he'd said, 'No,' which seemed like an invitation.

'Dad and Uncle Jim used to play it when they were teenagers,' I told him. 'They'd invented it, or something.'

My brother said, 'So what is it?'

I said, 'It's when you're driving and you close your eyes for five–'

'Oh yeah,' said my brother. 'I didn't realise it had a name.'

'Well, that's all thanks to me,' I said. 'I used to play it when we went shooting.'

'How?'

'I held the barrel of the .410 under my chin and counted to five.'

'With your finger on the trigger?'

'That's right.'

'I wish you hadn't just told me that.'

'Two miles until our junction,' I said. 'Want to have a go?' My brother plugged his phone into the aux cable, selected Burning Bridges by The Mike Curb Congregation and pressed play. I closed my eyes. 'Count to five,' I heard a young girl say.

My brother said this wasn't fun.

'This isn't funny,' he told me.

I was already on two-point-three.

From somewhere behind me my dead sister said, 'Three.'

My brother tried to reach over and take hold of the steering wheel, but I pushed his arm away.

'Four.'

'Open your fucking eyes,' he shouted.

'Five,' she yelled.

I opened my eyes but it was too late. We'd drifted onto an exit I hadn't prepared for. The speedometer was years past caring. The sound the engine made said EIGHTY.

It wasn't the Five Second Game that killed my older brother.

It was my decision to play it.

It was the speed at which we hit that corner.

And it was the rain, which caught the back wheels of the old Toyota and flicked the tail sideways. If you enter a spin, steer inwards. I knew this. It was the impact of my brother's head against the windscreen and the crushing force of the crushed cab ceiling which killed him. Not the fire which melted him, which is some consolation. There were no airbags. Wouldn't have mattered. The cab had partially collapsed. When the tail flicked out I did steer into it, but the car hit the barrier at the side of the slip road which rose quickly up an embankment to a roundabout and a bridge over the motorway. And with its wide wheel base and high off-road ground clearance the Toyota rode straight up and over that barrier.

Which is roughly when the bicycle started flying through the air.

In slow motion.

The Mike Curb Congregation, Burning Bridges, on the stereo, cutting back and forth between us in the car, turning over and over, and the bicycle finally hitting the ground.

Alright.

It ends–

Alright.

–with a crack–

Alright.

–as my head–

Alright.

–hits the window.

THE FIVE SECOND GAME – PART TWO (CONTINUED)

To field-strip your Mauser Kar98K you do this: rotate the cleaning rod (located beneath the barrel at the end of the forestock). Extract. Use the end of the cleaning rod to remove the magazine base plate (located in front of the trigger guard). Insert the cleaning rod. Depress the cleaning rod. Pull the cleaning rod to the rear. Remove the magazine base plate and the magazine assembly. When the magazine base is empty the bolt assembly locks. Turn the safety catch to the safe position (not the extra-safe position) and pull the bolt stop (located on the left side of the bolt assembly) out. Then slide the bolt casing from the receiver.

Depress the bolt lock on the bolt casing and rotate. Slide the bolt assembly and firing pin out of the bolt casing. Take the magazine base plate and insert it into the extractor (located on the bolt face). Turn anti-clockwise. Insert the bolt assembly and firing pin into the disassembly tool (embedded in the rear stock). Pull down and lift off the cocking piece. Then the safety catch. Then the pin spring.

And, finally, remove the firing pin.

Use a pull-through to clean dirt, residue and fingerprints from all metal parts. Reverse the process to reassemble. Oil to finish.

*

'Why that particular rifle?' said my sister, spinning shark-like in my wheel chair while I looked down from the thirteenth floor to the empty space where the paramedics and brief cases had been. I said, 'My father took us to a regimental museum once. It was our grandfather's regiment. There was no one else in there and the man on the door gave us a personal tour and took some of the rifles out of their cabinets. One was a Bren. One was a Mauser that'd been captured by the regiment and kept as a trophy. Also, I used to use it a lot when I played Call of Duty.'

The Mauser Kar98K (Karabiner) chambers the Mauser 7.9x57mm cartridge. Rimless and bottlenecked. With an effective range of up to 500 metres and a 2,000 metre mark on the rear sight (if you're feeling lucky).

'Are you feeling lucky?' asked my sister, dead (could be deader).

'I'm a good shot,' I told her. 'Don't you remember when we joined the Army Cadets?'

'It was a fling,' she'd said.

She stopped spinning. 'I remember you dragging me there.'

'I didn't want to go either,' I said.

'I remember you dragging me along,' she said, 'although I will admit that I did, and do still, quite want to see you in a hole in the ground.'

The doctors and nurses and paramedics and board members with brief cases smoking cigarettes by the ambulance entrance were no more than 100 metres away. Five rounds is not a lot. The Mauser Kar98K is renowned for its accuracy but not its rate of fire.

BANG.

And they'd almost certainly have a good chance to scatter.

'Do you remember when we visited the Army Air Corps for a day?' I said to my sister. 'We practised marching and we practised shooting on their range.'

She rolled her eyes. 'I remember one of the cadets taking part of his toe off with a blank round,' she said. 'Do you think he'd

done it on purpose, like Dad?'
I didn't reply.

After we'd burned down the barn I'd wanted to get my hands on a real grenade. The Air Corps instructors didn't know that I'd done all this already. In a past life. A legacy. My boots were too big for me. German paratrooper boots. Wide base. Flat feet. My mother never met my father's eye when I put on the parade tie or the camouflage jacket. Rubbed the scars on her arms and wrote a shopping list instead.

'I'm surprised you can stand already,' said my sister. 'How many days has it been? They must've used pretty strong pins. Expensive pins. I suppose you'll have to decide if the titanium holding you together is worth more than your brother's life. Not to mention whether, now, our mother wishes she'd left you alone to dig your own hole, with a rifle rather than a steering wheel.' My sister laughed. A man in hospital scrubs and Crocs was hugging a woman. He gave her a cigarette and she wiped her eyes. Someone was eating a salad pot on the steps leading up to the door. A dog was tied to a railing, looking anxious. The man in the heavy excavator was taking a tabloid newspaper into a tall, green, portable toilet. My sister said, 'When will she be here?'
She meant our mother.
Someone was walking towards us. I could hear their footsteps approaching and I imagined their eyes, raised to heaven as they followed the coloured lines or, maybe, glued to strange information on a clipboard. 'They're coming for you,' said my sister, who'd stood up. 'Better get back in this wheelchair.'

I CAN FEEL MY FATHER DYING

He started dying long ago. Shot through and hanged and plucked and cut up until he resembled something new, but not better. Better dead, my father always said. Better that, than in some home. But which home he meant was never specified. He never left the end-of-terrace house in front of the field with the abandoned concrete reservoir. He never wasn't there. Whistling up the stairs. Cleaning shotguns on the dining room table. Leaving cartridges on the dresser, in preparation for an intruder he could shoot and defeather. Hang for three days. Pluck, like he plucked my mother, then diced into one of her cakes.

He'd wait by the landline, clutching the address book with the rose petal cover and our surname embossed like brail or scar tissue, as if to prove that we existed; that the family he'd created could be as legitimate as the names that'd been listed in the book itself. Names that met other people for drinks on a Friday. Names he remembered from boarding school and had contacted in an attempt to refind old friendships, but which had long since become unobtainable to the likes of him. Bewildered unavailability mistaken for rejection. A personal shanking below the lowest, most pointless rib bone, at a 75 degree angle. The knife just kissing the lung. Oxygen exiting slowly for an agonising and lowly death.

My father is an inner tube. Rubber cracked and slapped across the face of his mother, who was unable to cut the bailer twine that dead creatures dangled from, on her Keep Calm and Carry On porch. Instead she coughed up a tapeworm. Instead she lost her mind. It walked off with her husband's medals, born down the aisle of a church and cushioned by a flag. Suffered for, bled for, amputated for and, instead of rationally abhorred, wept for.

Ding ding.

Every Fox is a Rabid Fox

My father rang the bells.

My father calls me. His remaining son has become a series of biro-dug crosses on those tea-stained treasure map address book pages. All the rest, or at least most, have been entrenched by a man grasping his fountain pen so hard all the blood has rushed out of his knuckles, and the line of the word he is writing–

Fuck you.

–bends the nib and almost tears through the paper.

Fuck out of my life, will you?

He sits on his bones on his favourite bar stool, alone in the village pub, wrapping himself round a reconditioned 1st generation iPhone, stalking old school friends on Facebook but unsure which buttons to press.

'What took you so long to answer?'

'I didn't hear it, that's all.'

'You going deaf, boy?'

I just don't want to speak to you.

'I can't believe you would see me calling and not immediately pick up your phone.'

I feel septic.

'How're you?' he asks.

'Fine, got a cut that won't heal.'

I can hear him thinking, standing by the table in the hallway, slightly too wide now to get past comfortably. Notepad and pens. Drawer for some stamps. Everything covered in dust. 'How long's this been going on for?' he asks me.

'No Dad.'

'It's not your fault, remember. Your brother, I mean.'

'That's not–'

'What did you use?'

'Use?'

'How did you do it?'

'It was a chainring.'

'A chainring?' he says. 'A bloody chainring? That's such a dirty thing. What's the matter with you?'

'I was fixing mum's bike.'

'They gave it back to you?'

'That's right.'

'Ah.'

My father's eyeing his armchair and wondering how long it'll take before I hang up. 'I thought you meant you'd been harming yourself,' he says, laughing. 'You know, people used to ask your mother if she self-harmed. In fact, people would see these marks on her arms and they'd ask me if I knew what she was doing. "Baking cakes", I'd say. "Baking cakes all day", I'd tell 'em, "and not ones worth burning yourself for on the oven door!"'

A pause.

'I think they thought I did it.'

Another pause.

'They must've thought I hurt her. Yes. That's why no one round here speaks to me anymore. But I never hit her,' he says.

'I know that, Dad,' I say.

'Yeah.'

He coughs.

'Yeah,' says my father, stroking his chin. Pulling his fingertip over the embossed lettering of our surname and wondering what the time is. 'Your mother said you've quit your job.'

'I'll get a new one.'

'When your leg heals?'

'Yeah.'

I cough.

'Well, uh, farmer's asked me to get rid of this fox for him. Been stealing his pheasant. Burying them with their feet poking out the ground in one of his fields. Anyway, you could help me, if you–'

'Have you spoken to Stephanie?'

*

My father hangs up the phone. He hangs up himself with some twine on the porch. I could go, I suppose. We could hang there, together. Ageing. Inedible. Making feathery small talk while we try to mature. While he anticipates the train that will take me away again, and I, failing to meet his eye, silently wait for the bailer twine to snap. Crack my kneecaps on the floor. Blood sprayed on the door to dry brown.

I go into the kitchen and find my little sister underneath the sink. She's drinking from a bottle of bleach. I say, 'That's a child safety cap,' and point to the child safety cap on the floor. 'How'd you get it off?'

She burps.

She says, 'You know me,' and offers the bottle.

'What do you want me to say?' says my sister, perusing the ashtray by the sofa. 'That everyone was already mourning? That one more death wouldn't transport them to a place they weren't already in and prepared to come back from?'

'You're not my friend,' I tell her. 'I don't want anything from you.'

'I'm not your enemy, either,' she says. 'I'm much worse than that. I'm your family.'

'Then why can't I ignore you?'

She smiles. 'You're still afraid he's living through you,' she says.

'Who?'

'He sounded surprisingly cheerful on the phone.'

'Oh.'

'As though you may actually go visit him.'

'I don't know.'
'Could be fun.'
'No.'
'Like a game.'
'I can't.'
'Count to five.'

I could burn it down. Stand at the side of the road below the gate. Below the pathway that divides the front garden. Watch it burn. Watch it turn into ash you can pinch with your thumb and forefinger then sprinkle around like salt. My sister, listing on the reef of my sofa, says, 'No.'

I say, 'Oh.'

She says, 'It's not as simple as setting fire to unwanted property. And besides,' pausing to yawn, 'you may actually get done for arson if you stand there holding the match.' She takes a long sip of bleach. 'You need to find out what really happened to Gentleman Jim. Have you ever, actually, thought about what it feels like to linger like he did? Like our grandmother still is?' My sister nudges another inch closer to my end of the sofa, touches her nose on my knee, puts her hand on my thigh and squeezes. 'You'll just be killing a fox,' she says, quietly.

WILLOW

Willow messages me. We haven't spoken since she left my house that night. Something going. Something off. Again. Doesn't matter. Didn't matter, then, when we broke up before. She's been calculating. I imagine. Needs to decide whether I'm a good idea. I don't think so. Doesn't matter still. She messages in the morning, wants to meet for coffee. Sounds awfully familiar. 'Are you sure this is a good idea?' I say, packing bag. Locking up. Takes a lot to drop the last washing up in the bowl. Peanut butter spoon, though, is all. I've been subsisting. Now everything's empty. 'I'm going to see Stephanie,' I text her, stepping out of the door with my sister on the floor, in a bag. 'You can meet me before I go.'

Willow, with a coffee. Willow, toffee hair and early-morning-just-brushed-teeth breath but things are yellow. Stained iodine. Things have never not been tainted. Willow with the dread of caffeine-pissing. We're in Liverpool Street Station and Willow says, 'This coffee's terrible. Why couldn't we meet somewhere else?'

'I've got to catch a train.'

'We could've met sooner.'

'You're the one who disappeared,' I say. 'You've not spoken to me for days, so why does it matter?'

She says, 'I'm sorry.'

She says, 'You're not well.'

'Do you think you took advantage of me?' I ask.

Willow looks at me. Willow's angry. Willow says, 'Don't you dare.'

I say, 'Sorry. That was stupid.' Pause. 'You're not missing out, anyway,' I tell her. 'How's your boyfriend?'

'He's not my boyfriend.'

'What happened?'

'Nothing.'

'It's just that you've dyed your hair again.'

For a moment she's quiet, then says, 'I need the toilet.'

'They're pretty clean here, this early.' Looking towards the bar. Fake wooden casks panel-pinned to the wall. 'You don't even have to buy anything.'

Willow leaves.

Willow comes back.

Willow says, 'Why are you going to see Stephanie?'

'The same reason you came here for this bad coffee,' I say. 'To apologise.'

I smile.

'Is it really that easy for you?' she says. 'To clench your jaw and be a dick and act like you're fine, when everything must be tearing you up inside?'

'You didn't seem to mind last week. Or the week before that.'

'It wasn't right,' she says. 'I thought I was helping. No, I don't mean it like that.'

'It's fine.'

'Stop saying that.'

'You've got a boyfriend.'

'Is that what you want? To be with me again?'

'I want to forget.'

There's a pause. Spoons clatter somewhere behind. Commuter overflow. Somewhere, an announcement caught in the throes of goodbye.

'I spoke to your mother the other day,' says Willow.

I say, 'I know.'

'You need to go see her.'

She touches my knee.

'Wouldn't it be better,' says Willow, 'rather than seeing your sister-in-law, to get some therapy? Get your head in the right place? You haven't seen Stephanie since–'

'I'm going to see my father, too.'

'How long will you be?'

I don't answer.

'That's good,' says Willow. 'But wouldn't it make more sense to see your mother and Stephanie at the same time, since they both live near each other?'

'I don't know, Willow,' I say angrily, scooping milk froth out of a tiny enamel jug on the table. 'This is just how I've planned it. And anyway, why does it matter?'

Willow opens her bag. Takes out a small case. Opens that. Takes out a packet. Puts a pill in her mouth and swallows. 'Want me to get you a glass of water?' I ask.

She says, 'I'm fine.'

My bag on the floor starts to shake. It's almost time. Struggling to look her in the eye. Now who's guilty? 'You've got to stop saying that,' I say. Willow smiles. I feel relaxed. It doesn't–

Willow shouts. 'Don't you think you'd be coping better if you'd just fucking SCREAM? If you'd let yourself CRY?'

The bag on the floor is unzipping itself.

'You're infuriating,' she says. 'And I don't know what to do.'

'There's no use in worrying,' I tell her.

Something dark, twisted. Something bitter slides out. A shadow. I don't follow it. I can see the clock in the foyer. I can see my sister standing under it.

'What would you have done if you had been pregnant?' I say.

'I would have got an abortion.'

'Exactly.'

I zip the bag back up.

'And if your brother died,' I ask, 'then what?'

'Well I wouldn't go around fucking apologising for it,' says Willow.

I stand. Shift the brown polyester chair to the side.

'Actually,' I say, shouldering my bag, 'you'd wait. Then, eventually, you'd follow him.'

I HAVE THOUGHT ABOUT POISONING YOU

'Perfect,' says my sister, washing her hands in the basin while we're looking at ourselves in Stephanie's bathroom mirror. 'That was perfect,' while she sat on Stephanie's toilet with her knickers round her ankles. 'I almost can't believe it,' when I locked the door behind us and stood at the window and waited. 'She really bought it,' as we sped towards Chelmsford, in need of a piss.

'How did you come up with that?' she said only a few hours ago. 'That bit about following your brother? Frankly, I'm surprised at you.'

'I feel cruel.'

'Don't worry about it,' she said. 'She'll forget all about you.'

*

Stephanie met us at the station. I'd told her she didn't have to, but she insisted. She said, 'We're still family, aren't we? And anyway, I'm going to be the mum-taxi at some point. May as well start practising.'

Her son, not yet two, was sitting on the back seat.

Her son was thinking about poisoning me.

That's what he looked like.

I said, 'Sorry to drag you out here, too.'

He smiled, but didn't say anything.

'Do you find it fun?' says my sister, dead, half-in-and-out of the toilet as she tries to pull her knickers up. 'Playing people off against one another?'

I've been standing in front of the mirror for almost 20 minutes.

'Are you alright in there?' says Stephanie, tapping gently on the old bathroom door.

The floor is cold. Orange tiles. The smile of her firstborn is a thousand miles from his future, when he'll be old enough to come to terms with the death of his father. If he even remembers him. Outside, the rhododendrons need a trim.

'I was thinking of getting a man in, actually,' Stephanie tells me, gathering her unborn second baby and standing in front of the open French window. 'Is that the Virgin Mary on the mantel piece?' I ask.

'Oh, it's just something I've gotten used to,' she says, then looks at me. 'Are you feeling alright?'

'Fine, thank you,' I say. 'Too much coffee on the train.'

There's a pause.

'I could do it, maybe,' I say, looking at the overgrown bush. Cut it back, then burn the roots.'

*

I've spent this afternoon destroying the rhododendron bush. Stephanie suggested I stop halfway. Getting late. Have some food. Stephanie said that she could finish it herself, and I knew she could but she had my nephew to look after. He wasn't doing much, except staring at the corner where my dead little sister sat staring straight back. I said no. Not hungry. Thank you. 'I wonder where the cat's gone?' says Stephanie, but I don't answer. Saw the cat before, pulling in. Got out of the car. Extended its claws in the driveway. Fur stood up as my dead sister walked into the house. 'She must've gone off into the woods.'

'Would you like me to check the workshop?' I ask, with a long birch branch underarm and a pair of gardening gloves. 'She may be hiding in there.'

'Well, I usually keep it locked, now,' says Stephanie. 'I don't think she'd have been able to get in.' She looks at me. And looks at me. Sudden, sad, happy frown. 'But you know what cats are like, eh?' she says. 'Wait here while I get the key,' batting rhododendron tendrils and severed branch limbs out of the way.

My brother's workshop is inside a curved, corrugated iron building, by a dried-up old yew tree at the end of the garden. My brother put it up himself, coated it with primer then a layer of matt black paint which, by now, is peeling. Revealing layers of red. Stephanie gave me a key to the workshop then said she'd go inside to make up the spare bed. She left quickly.

The air inside the workshop smells of oil and metal and wood smoke. The carcasses of old motorbikes hide the marks left when my brother used to get frustrated and throw spanners at the walls. A thick, greasy bike chain hangs from a hook by the window, which is filthy and decorated with cobwebs, while the tiny wood-burning stove, with which he made tea in the corner, looks colder than the little girl's leg poking out of it.

I rush to grab it.

'What the HELL are you doing in here?'

My sister screams.

'WHAT THE HELL do you think you are doing?'

I try pulling her out, grab, pull. But she's half-stuck in the under-insulated chimney flue. Pull again, white knuckle pain on the door catch and when she bursts out brings a coughing-fit soot cloud. My sister, raggedy, says, 'I was just trying to tidy a bit.' Then she trips over an empty oil canister. Coughs some more. Says, 'Thought I'd start with this old thing here,' patting the chimney. 'They're dangerous, you know. Houses burn down because families don't clean out their soot.'

'No one's lighting it up here,' I tell her.

'Everything alright?' It's Stephanie. Standing in the doorway, her unborn baby spinning around. 'Oh, sweetheart,' she says to me when I face her. 'Here, take this.' She hands me a small, dark-blue handkerchief. 'I tend to keep it with me, these days. Seems a waste to keep buying tissues. But I've got a couple more, anyway, so you keep that one, eh?'

I touch my face.

'Don't worry,' she says, 'it's clean.'

I hadn't realised that there were tears all over me.

'Are you going to tell her the truth?' my sister asks me, dropping more soot on the floor and blowing soot in my face and breathing impatient cough-soot, while Stephanie stands still in the door and just looks. And just looks. And just looks.

For a long time we stand and say nothing.

Just nothing.

It is easier this way.

Then, eventually, I spoil the world and say, 'Well, the cat's not here, anyway.' Wipe my face with the handkerchief she gave me. Try gently to nudge her out of the way so I can leave, but Stephanie stops me.

Stephanie looks at me.

Stephanie says, 'It's okay.'

Trying to look, look into me, my eyes.

'It's okay.'

It comes: 'Is it?'

Momentously long pause.

'Is it, really?'

'Come here,' she tells me. Commands. I always liked that about her. So I do. Go there, towards her in the door frame. Arms out. Doorway. Cobwebs and bike chain. And then my arms around her and hers around me and my head in her shoulder and my heart in her throat and my eyes like levees broke like nope nope nope don't say it.

'Just do it,' shouts my sister.

'I–'

'FASTER.'

'I killed him.'

'Don't say that,' says Stephanie.

'But it's true.'

I don't know if I can believe her. It's only been a few months. I'm still struggling to walk. Stephanie puts her son to bed while I make us a couple of drinks. 'A weak one won't hurt the baby,' she says. Rubs her belly. Takes a kitchen chair and the G&T I've made her out onto the lawn by the smoking remains of the rhododendron bush. 'Still no sign of the cat,' she says.

'She'll probably come back when we leave,' I say.

'Hmm?'

'She'll be back when she's hungry. Don't worry. She's a young cat. She still has all her lives left.'

'It's the fox that worries me,' says Stephanie. 'He's been stealing my chickens at night. He's been coming in through a hole in the fence, stealing my chickens and then burying them upside down, by the yew tree at the end of the garden, so only their feet poke out.'

'You going to kill him?' I say.

'Maybe he's a she,' says Stephanie. 'Maybe she's got babies to feed every day, too.'

There's a pause. Stephanie stirs the ash of the rhododendron bush with her foot. 'I'm not going to kill her,' she says. 'I'm going to keep repairing the fence.'

'Who do you think your baby's going to look like, this time?'

'Like Luke, I hope,' says Stephanie. She takes a sip of gin. 'I'm going to name him after his dad, anyway.'

'So they tell you it's a boy again?'

'Of course it's a boy.' She nudges my shoulder and I smile. 'You mustn't let me forget to give you some eggs before you leave,' she says.

I shake my head and say, 'You keep them.'

AN INVITATION TO THE DEATH OF A FOX

There's a missed call on my phone from my mother. There's a half-eaten burger in front of the TV. And one eye of my father is roving me. I took a cab from the station to my old family home. It took me six numbers and seventeen minutes to find one. The reception isn't kind, this side of London. It's all dial tones and landlines. Endlessly ringing answering machine wind chimes. One lady said, simply, 'We don't do that anymore,' then hung up. I almost phoned Willow, who would've had 4G, but stopped myself and went to see what business cards they had inside the train station. The ticket office was closed. The ticket office was always closed. I don't remember it ever having been open. Rainy, red-brick holes for windows. Waiting room abandoned. Boarded up. Tickets torn up and dropped on the floor around clear plastic bin bags, but not in them. My father knew I was coming, but the whole thing felt like a show.

I found a taxi driver shouting at another car in the rank. Bookings only. Official passes passable to parking officers, but where they were the bemused other-driver couldn't tell. When I went over, to interrupt, I could hear him trying to explain that he was only waiting for his daughter.

Throat deep in mayonnaise my father says, 'So tell me.' He says that and nothing more.

'The driver told me, "Bookings only,"' I say.

We're eating early. Well, he's eating. I'm picking. Not flicking through channels. Doesn't matter what we watch. 'I could see the taxi office from where he was shouting. I had to go over and ask for a taxi, and then I had to wait five minutes. And when they told me, "He's arriving now," it was the same driver I'd just spoken to.'

My father nods.

My little sister's curled up where the dog used to sleep.

'You spoken to your mother?' he says.

'A little.'

'She still living in Essex?'

'Uh huh.'

'You should see her before you find another job and get too busy to visit us again.'

'Maybe.'

My father nods.

I clear the plates. Kitchen's a mess. Father says, 'Thought we might take the guns out tomorrow.' He's rolling a cigarette. 'Bag a few birds while we look for that fox's den.'

'Didn't know you smoked,' I say.

He nods.

'Okay.'

'Okay what?'

'Let's take the guns out.'

My sister looks up.

'I've still got that old .410, you know,' says my father.

'I thought you'd sold it.'

The bin is overflowing.

'No. I've been popping rats at that new barn they've built. You still hungry?'

I look at what's left of the burger on my plate. Soggy from microwave. Sweaty pillow for bun. Kebab dream meat patty and mystery cheese. I say, 'No.' Open the fridge for some juice.

'Sorry about the smell,' says my father. 'I haven't had time to mend the broken seal. Here,' he says, getting up and walking over, 'I bought a cake for pudding, if you like.' Before I can answer he's already cutting me a slice. Elbowing around a kitchen that used to feel a lot bigger. 'Carrot's your favourite, right? Carrot's your favourite? I know it's not homemade, but I'm sure it'll taste alright. I've got some work to do in the village tomorrow afternoon. Bit of plumbing at the church hall. But if you'd like to take the guns out, the morning's free.' My sister coughs loudly, expecting a treat. 'Though, they could do with a clean.'

*

'There's newspaper by the Parkray,' says my father. 'Put the newspaper on the table and–'

'Some on the floor?' I say. 'I know. I remember.'

My father takes a key from the dresser by the wall bracket TV and opens the door to the cupboard under the stairs where the gun cabinet is bolted. He brings out two cleaning kits. One for the .410 and one for the 12 bore. They're in long thin cardboard cases, the 12 bore case slightly thicker, its edges worn, one corner torn, and an elastic band round the middle to keep its guts together. My father lays them on the newspaper I placed on the table then goes back to the cupboard. 'Spoken to Stephanie lately?' he asks me.

'I saw her yesterday, actually.'

'How's she getting on?'

'She seems fine. How do you think?'

He brings out the shotguns. Lays them next to the long thin boxes on the newspaper on the table. 'Just a second,' he says, going back for the old can of Youngs 303.

'How's the baby?'

'Which one.'

'The one that's been born.' He shakes his head.

'Quiet,' I say. 'Looks more and more like him every day.'

My father nods. 'Can't be easy.'

'She's cracking on,' I say. 'Keeping busy.'

My father nods.

He sits down.

'She's got a fox,' I tell him, standing up from my chair to get a glass of water from the kitchen where, speaking louder, I say, 'keeps stealing her chickens.'

'She going to kill him?' he asks.

'No. And it might be a she.'

My father shakes his head. 'She's a fool there,' he says. 'If she doesn't kill him, or at least get someone else to kill him, he'll end up taking every chicken she owns.'

I sit down at the table and face him. 'Probably. But even if she does,' I say, 'one of its children will just do the same.'

My father rests his hands on a shotgun. 'You've got to shoot them all, I'm afraid.'

There's a pause.

'Look here,' he says, pointing at the newspaper I placed open on the table, 'Kelly's Heroes is on Channel Five tomorrow.' He sniffs. 'Shall we watch it? Haven't seen that in years.'

I smile, tell him, 'I'd love to.'

'Good,' says my father, smiling too. 'Now, to field-strip your shotgun, you–'

GETTING AWAY WITH ARSON

I get up early for breakfast. When I come downstairs from my old bedroom I find my father near the kitchen, by the cupboard under the stairs where the shotguns and camouflage clothing and cartridges have always been kept. Busy man. Excitable. Putting on a pair of camouflage trousers that had once fitted but are now too large for him. His olive drab shirt is open. Grey chest hair. Sunken sternum. Makes me sad. When he sees me he says, 'I got yours out too, but I don't suppose they'll still fit you.' A small pile of clothes has been dumped on the armchair. They smell of soil and silage. Grease and cordite. Haven't been washed in years. 'Don't worry though,' says my father. 'Farmer's been cutting new footpaths but there're still plenty of bushes to hide in. And your hat,' he says, putting something brown on my head, 'looks fine. Your head always was rather large as a child.' He laughs. 'Here, take this,' chucking me a Barbour. 'Was your grandfather's, that.'

We walk up the zigzag track to the bend where I shot my first rabbit. There are no rabbits there today, so we walk a little further. The farmer has a hunch that the fox lives near the old concrete reservoir, so we head in that direction. And as we walk my father speaks a little, and speaks quietly. 'I spoke to Jim's solicitor,' he tells me. 'The, uh, Last Will and Testament is about to come through.'

'What could he have possibly left behind?' I ask.

My father sighs. 'Your uncle was never a rich man. He could've been. He was so smart. But he didn't care much about that kind of thing.'

'I expect he probably buried his riches somewhere.'

My father laughs. 'Not still going on about murder, are you?' he says. 'Jim was a debt collector. And then a very ill man.'

'Were you with him when he died?' I ask.

There's a pause.

It is a long pause.

It is made longer because my father has stopped walking. When the pause ends and he starts walking again my father says, 'Yes.' Then my father says, 'He didn't want to linger.' He puts his hand on my shoulder and we stop walking again. Just stand here facing each other on the track. Guns underarm. It's the first time I've seen him look like he's going to cry. He was stoic when my mother left him, and I didn't see him at my brother's funeral because I wasn't there. 'Do you understand?' he says.

My mouth's been open the whole time. My eyes a little too wide. 'You mean you–'

'It's fine.'

'How?'

'I helped him.'

'How?'

My father hugs me.

'He just went out for a little swim.'

At the top of the track we look in the field behind our house. The old concrete reservoir is still there. The elder tree is still beside it. The woods are further on. 'Usual drill,' says my father. 'I'll go to the top, try and flush some birds down to you at the bottom. Okay?' We start walking away from each other, but after about twenty metres I stop and I turn and I say, 'We did burn that barn down, you know.'

My father nods. 'I know, Robert,' he says. 'It just never bothered me.'

When I reach the hedgerow at the top of the down my dead little sister is there. She's been waiting for me all morning. 'Took your time,' she says. 'What did he say?'

'It doesn't matter.'

'Fine, don't tell me.' She's shrinking. She's getting ready to go back in. To be reabsorbed. I stand next to her in the hollowed out bush beneath the tree, she at once both my age and a child, a baby. 'Is it loaded?' she asks, pointing to the old .410 that had belonged to Gentleman Jim. Rustier now. Worn out old hammer and white paint flecks on the stock that someone, years ago, tried to scratch off.

My phone vibrates.

'Hold on,' I say. 'It's our mother.'

'What does she want?'

'She says she's sent me a Tesco delivery.'

My sister raises her eyes. 'The gun–'

'Yes, it's loaded,' I tell her, 'but the safety is on.'

'Turn it off,' she says.

I switch the safety off.

Click.

She says, 'Give that to me.'

I hand her my phone.

She throws it across the field. Wild flowers. Dry earth. The smell of burnt wood. I lower the handle and turn the gun upwards.

'Rest your–'

'Chin on the end of the barrel. Yes, I remember.'

The sound of church bells drifts up from the village.

I put my finger on the trigger.

'Good,' says my sister. 'Now, we're going to count to five.'

ACKNOWLEDGEMENTS

I'd like to thank Nathan Connolly and Amelia Collingwood at Dead Ink, Emily Harrison, for making me work harder, Aki Schilz, for her continuing guidance, Frank Brinkley, for giving his time and annotations, and The Authors' Foundation and The Society of Authors K Blundell Trust Award, for their recognition and encouragement.

Publishing the Underground

Publishing the Underground is Dead Ink's project to develop the careers of new and emerging authors. Supported by Arts Council England, we use our own crowdfunding platform to ask readers to act as patrons and fund the first run print costs.

If you'd like to support new writing then visit our website and join our mailing list. This book was made possible by kind contributions from the following people...

Mediah Ahmed
Lulu Allison
Chantelle Atkins
Rj Barker
Ella Beedham
Alex Blott
Naomi Booth
Julia Brich
Edward Burness
Daniel Carpenter
Craig Chalmers
Alan Clarkson
Sarah Cleave
Tracey Connolly
Nyle Connolly
Catriona Cox
Stuart Crewes
Steve Dearden
Vanessa Dodd
Jessica Easton
Jack Ecans
Su Edwards
Daniel Edwards
Laura Elliott
Lee Farley
Jesse May Fisher
Jack Flanagan
Naomi Frisby
Peter Gallon
Heidi Gardner
Sarah Garnham
Sophie Grant
Vince Haig
Paul Hancock
Emily Harrison
Judith Heneghan
Jan Hillman
Harriet Hirshman
Darren Hopes
Ross Jeffery
Haley Jenkins
Laura Jones

Haroun Khan
Lewis King
Simon Lee
Margaret McCormack
Heather McDaid
Chloe McLeod
Sam Mildner
Kiran Millwood Hargrave
Chris Naylor
Elliot Newton
Tom Nomico
Sophie Hopesmith
Jasmin Piercy
Ruth Pooley Ford
James Powell
Hannah Powley
Tom Preston
Sarah Pybus
Becky Radcliffe
Mal Ramsay
Gareth Rees
Liam Riley
Matthew Shenton
Alex Shough
Katie Sinclair
Nicky Smalley
Vicky Smith
Poppy Steveni
Julie Swain
Catherine Syson
Mia Tagg
Michael Thomson
Martina Toikka
Rupert Van Den Broek
Sally Vince
Stephen West
Emily Whitaker
Sara White
Anna White
Eley Williams
Edwin Wong
James Yeoman

About Dead Ink...

Dead Ink is a small, ambitious and experimental literary publisher based in Liverpool.

Supported by Arts Council England, we're focused on developing the careers of new and emerging authors.

We believe that there are brilliant authors out there who may not yet be known or commercially viable. We see it as Dead Ink's job to bring the most challenging and experimental new writing out from the underground and present it to our audience in the most beautiful way possible.

Our readers form an integral part of our team. You don't simply buy a Dead Ink book, you invest in the authors and the books you love.

Also from Dead Ink...

Guest
SJ Bradley

Samhain is a young, angry and bewildered squatter living in an abandoned hotel in the North of England. One day he receives a message: His father – a man he never knew – was an undercover policeman infiltrating the Green movement of the 80s. What's more, he finds out that he too is now a father.

As Sam leaves for Europe, he pursues freedom and flees from his responsibilities. Responsibility, however, is hard to escape. Guest is a story of disillusionment, protest and, eventually, redemption.

SJ Bradley is a writer from Leeds and one of the organisers behind Fictions of Every Kind. She won the Willesden Herald Short Story Prize and was shortlisted for the Gladstone Writers in Residency Award. Her debut novel, Brick Mother, was published by Dead Ink in 2014.

Another Justified Sinner
Sophie Hopesmith

It's the eve of the recession, but who cares? For commodity trader Marcus, life is good: he's at the top of the food chain. So what if he's a fantasist? So what if he wills his college sweetheart to death? So what if it's all falling apart? This isn't a crisis. Until it is.

As misfortune strikes again and again, he goes to help others and 'find himself' abroad – but it turns out that's not as easy as celebrities make it look on TV. Another Justified Sinner is a feverish black comedy about the fall and rise and fall of Marcus,an English psycopath. How difficult is it to be good?

Sophie Hopesmith is a 2012 Atty Awards finalist and her background is in feature writing. Born and bred in London, she works for a reading charity. She likes comedy, poetry, writing music, and Oxford commas. All of her favourite films were made in the 70s.

Harry Gallon

Harry Gallon's work features in numerous publications and has won (and almost won), several competitions. His debut novel, The Shapes of Dogs' Eyes (Dead Ink Books), was first runner up for Best Novella at the 2016 Saboteur Awards, and was longlisted for Not the Booker Prize 2016. He lives in London.